I0825309

Daylight

SYLVANIA

Anna Beeke

with words by Brian Doyle

Cofounders: Taj Forer and Michael Itkoff
Designer: Ursula Damm
Copy editor: Elizabeth Bell

ISBN 978-1-942084-05-1

Printed in China

Daylight Books
E-mail: info@daylightbooks.org
Web: www.daylightbooks.org

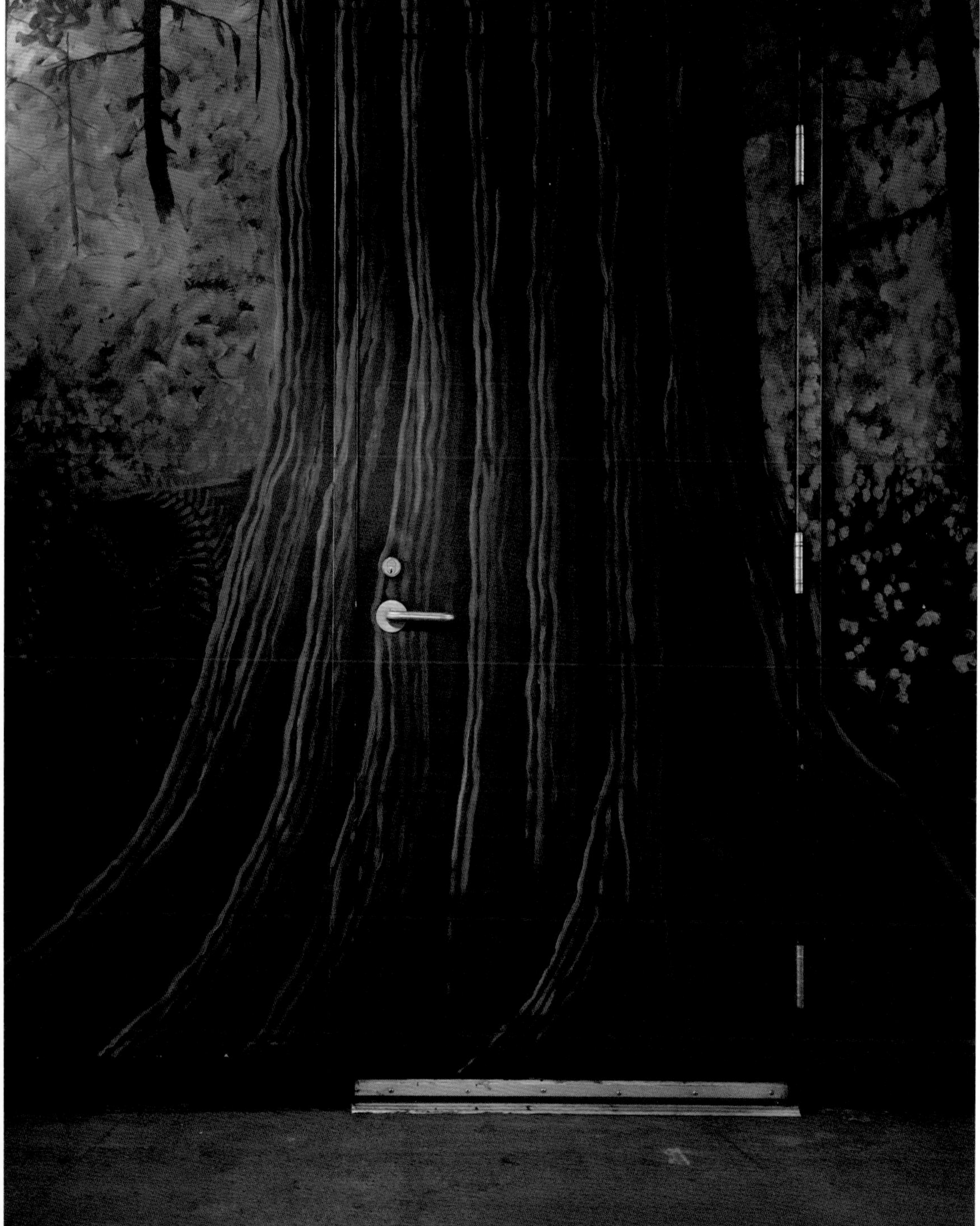

You could walk
into the woods
anywhere, any sort
of woods, every
sort of woods, and
you would be a
different animal
within ten steps,
as soon as the
woods accepted
you, as soon as
you couldn't hear
anything else but
the woods. We
forget that the
woods are always
there waiting. We
are afraid of the
woods and we
love the woods
and we used
to live in the
woods and some
part of us is still
fascinated and
frightened and
absorbed and
mesmerized
and yearning
secretly for
the woods. I
suppose there
will always be
woods in us
somehow until
there are no
more woods or
no more us. We came
from them as if from
a tangled green sea
and the parts of us
that are still mammal
are most comfortable
there. We forget we
are mammals. You
could walk into the
woods anywhere
and you would be
different within a
minute or two –
rattled, happier,
muddier, cautious,
more alert, home in
some way for which
we do not yet have an
excellent green word.

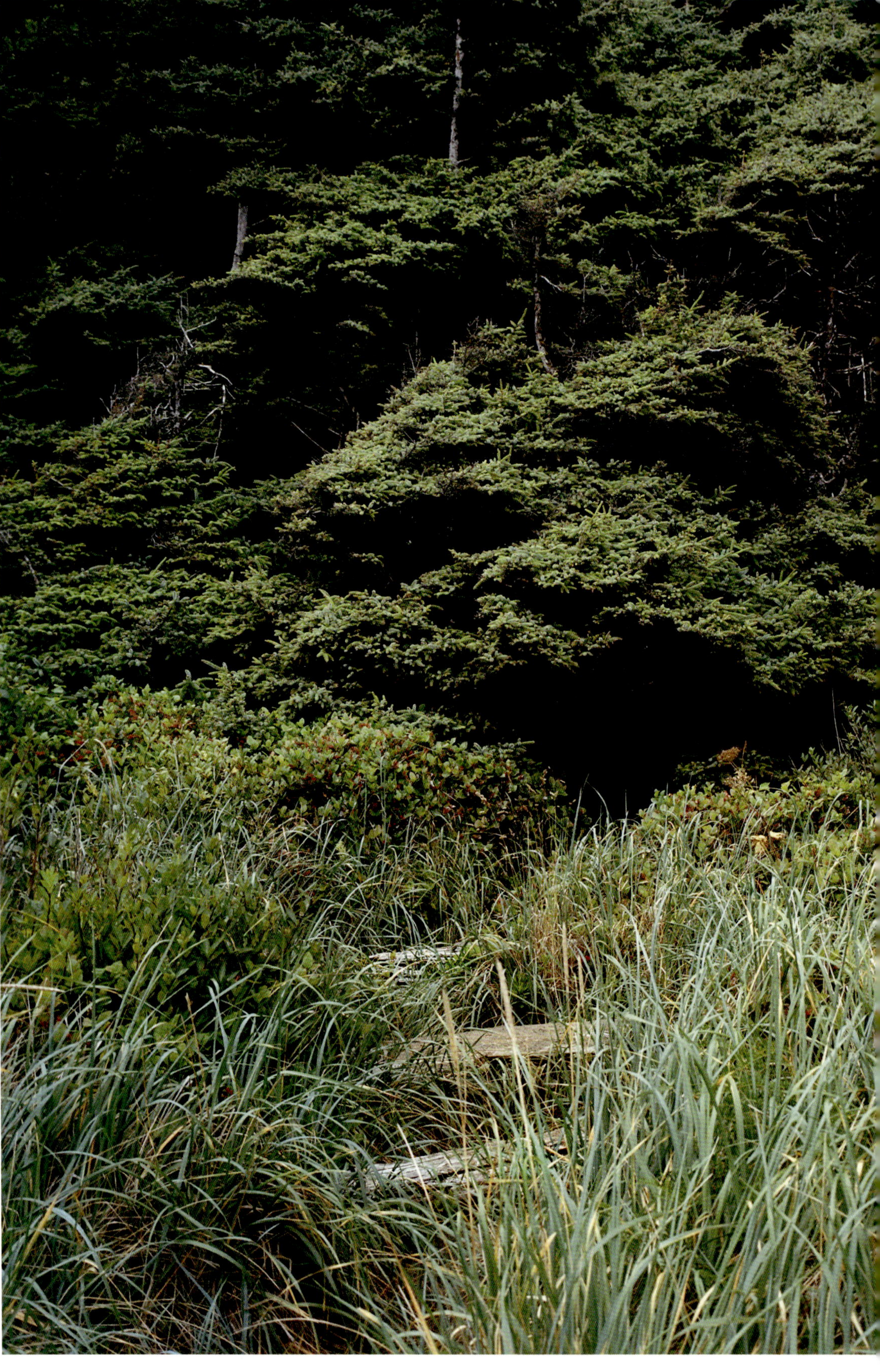

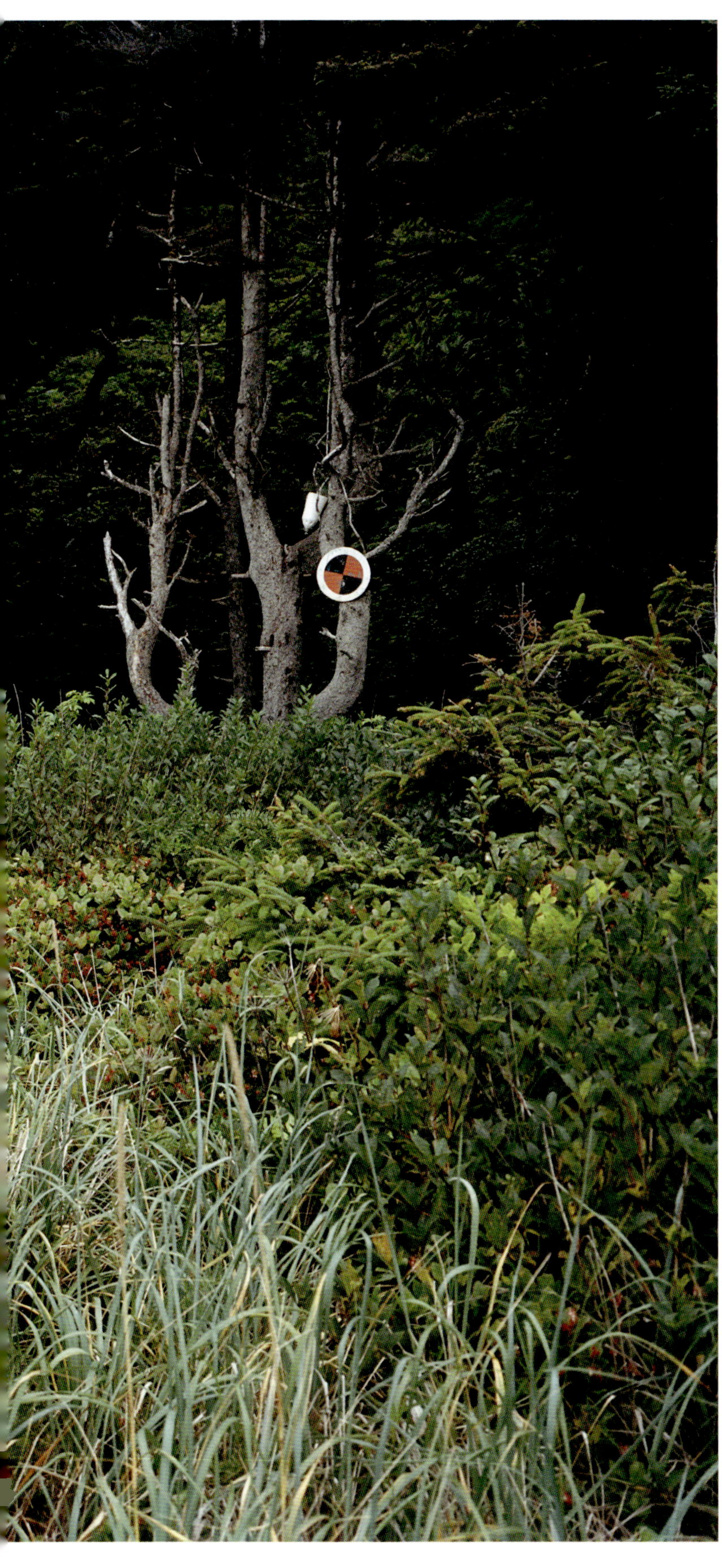

The densest place I have ever been in my whole life is deep in the woods here. One time I stood on what I thought was a small hillock but it turned out to be duff ten feet deep. There was a rumor of cougar. Of course it was raining. Of course it was. I sat down for a while and thought about all the languages that were being spoken and had been spoken in this one moist incredible place in the world, all the creatures of every kind who had lived here or passed through this space, the uncountable insects, the children, the young ones of every species. Had they gaped too, at the pillars of the trees, the bear print, the murmur of owls?

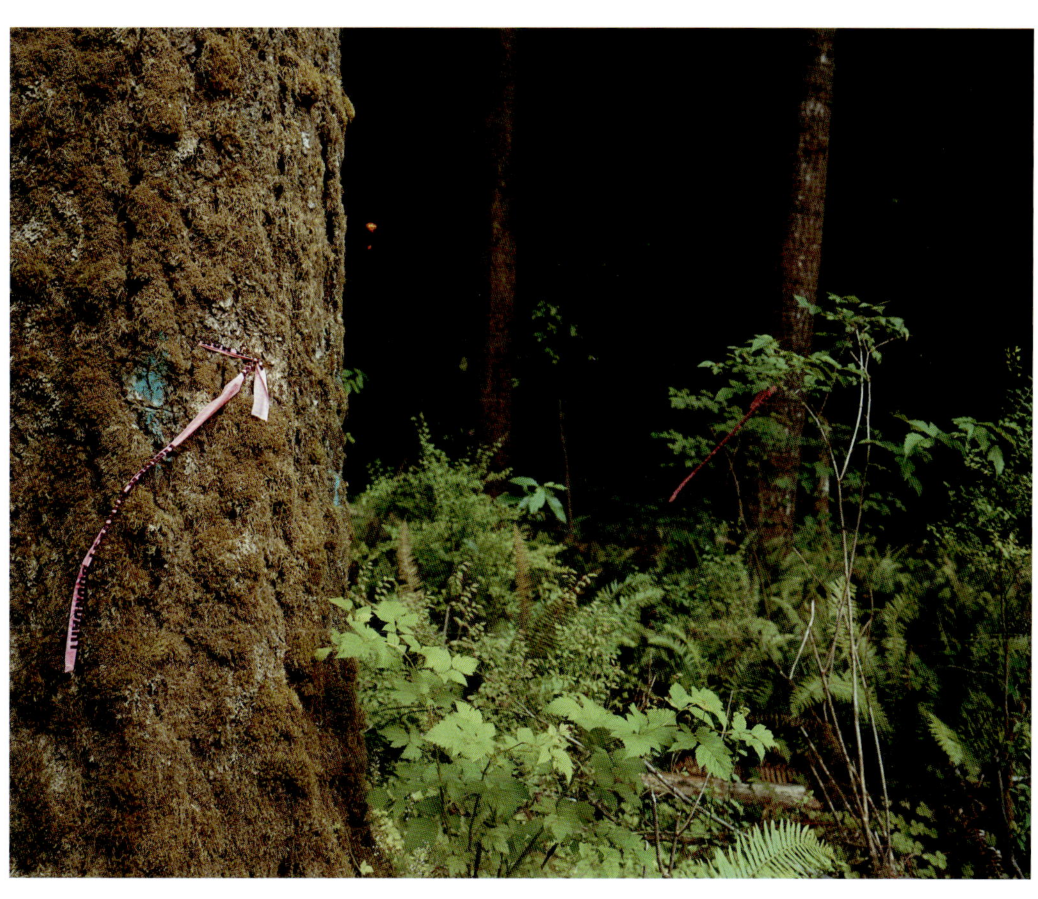

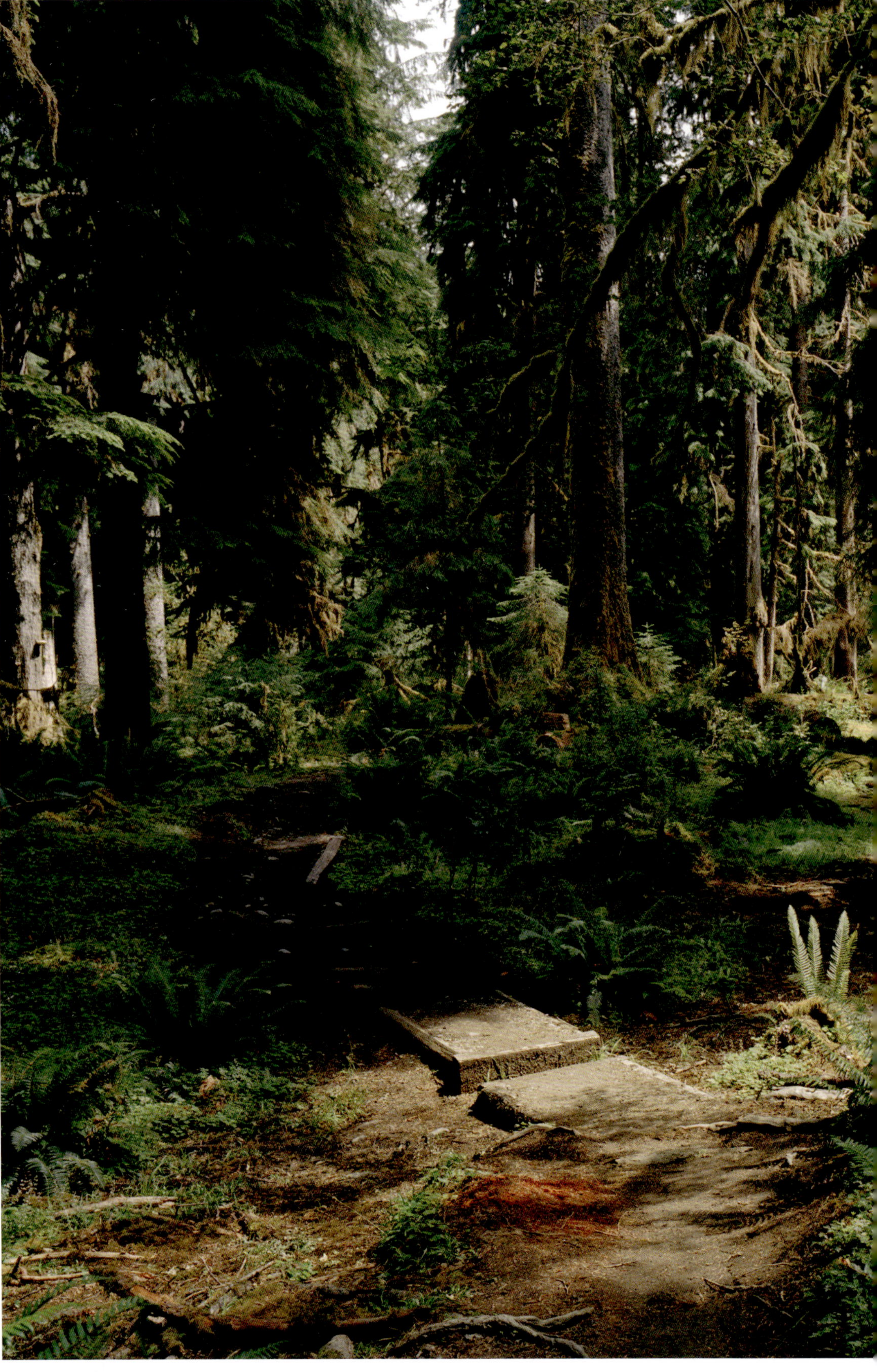

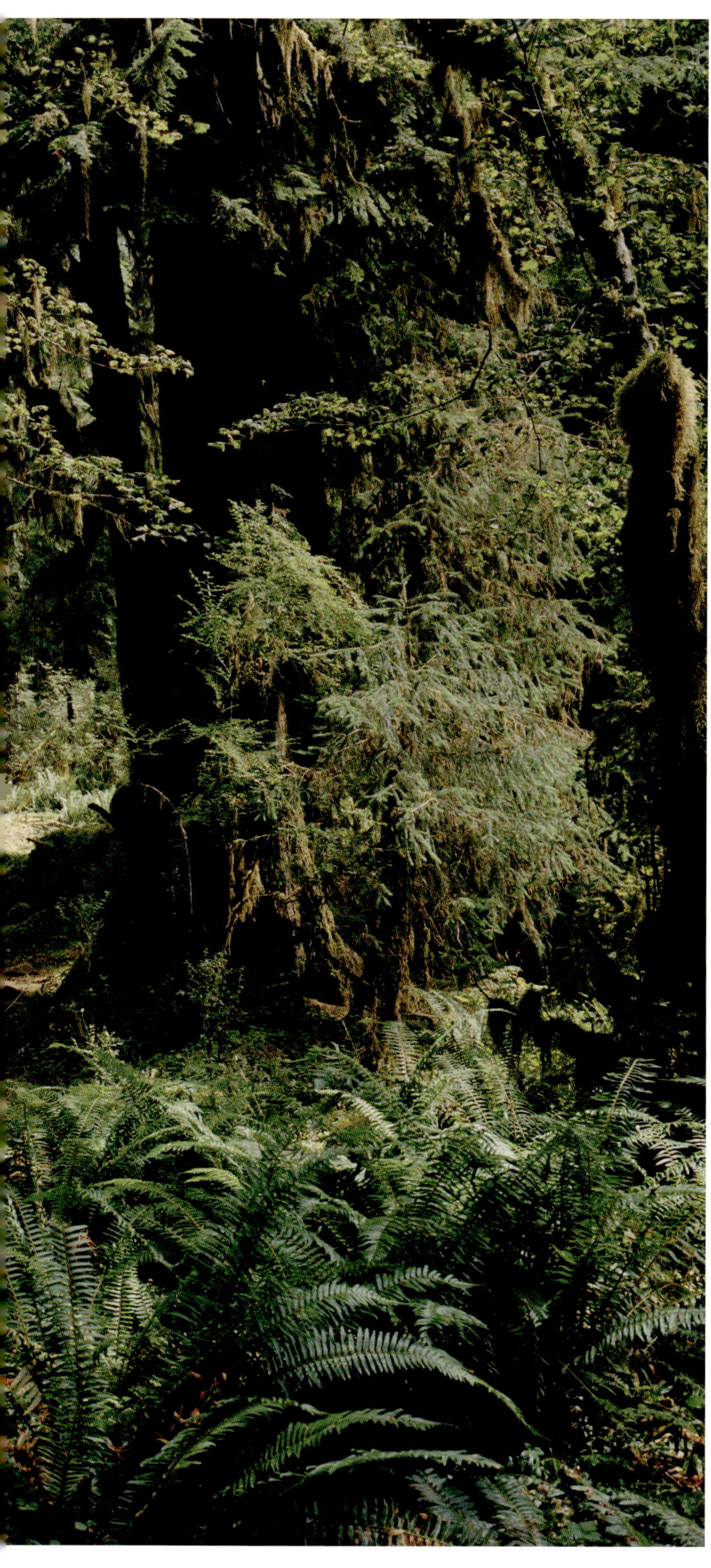

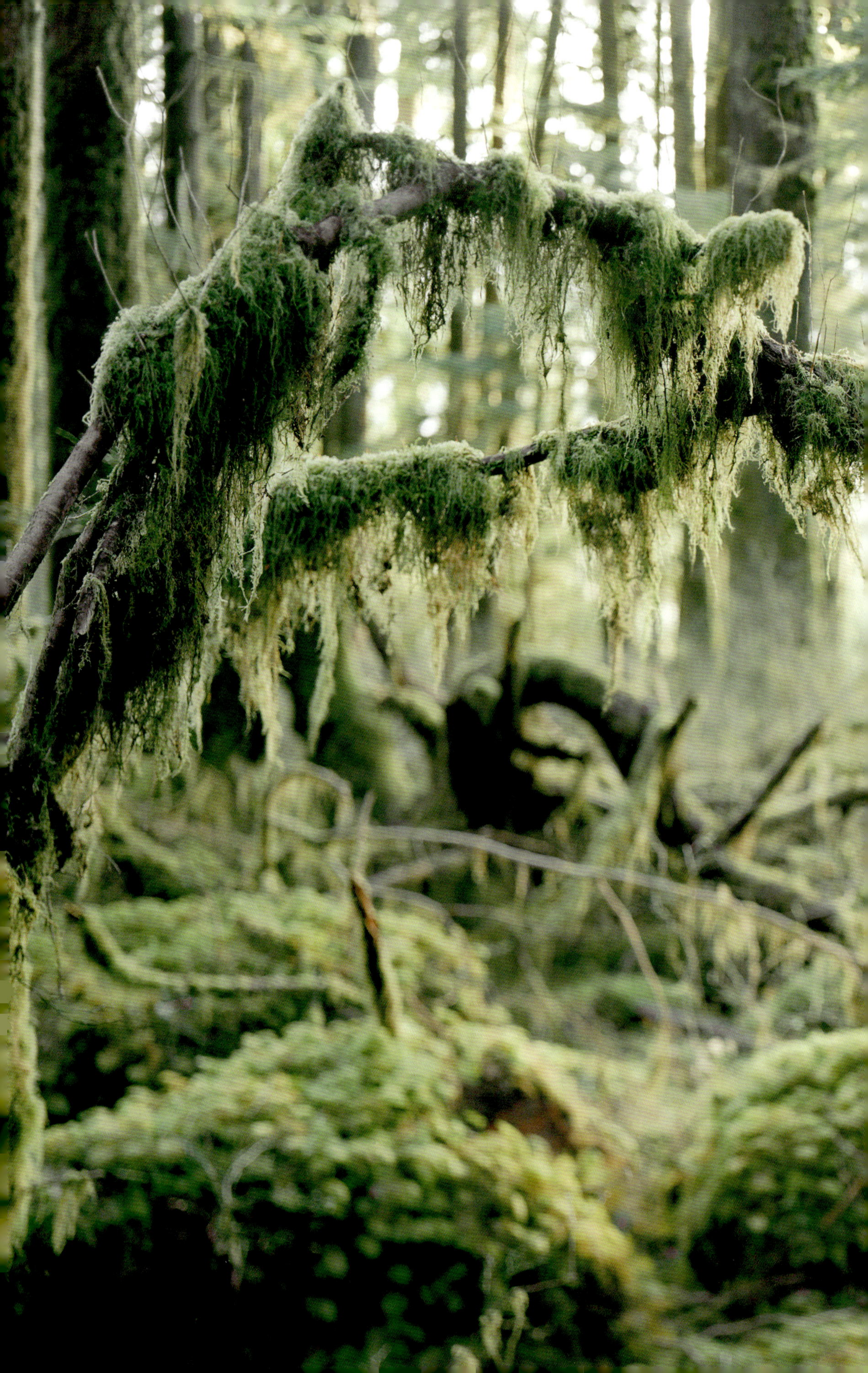

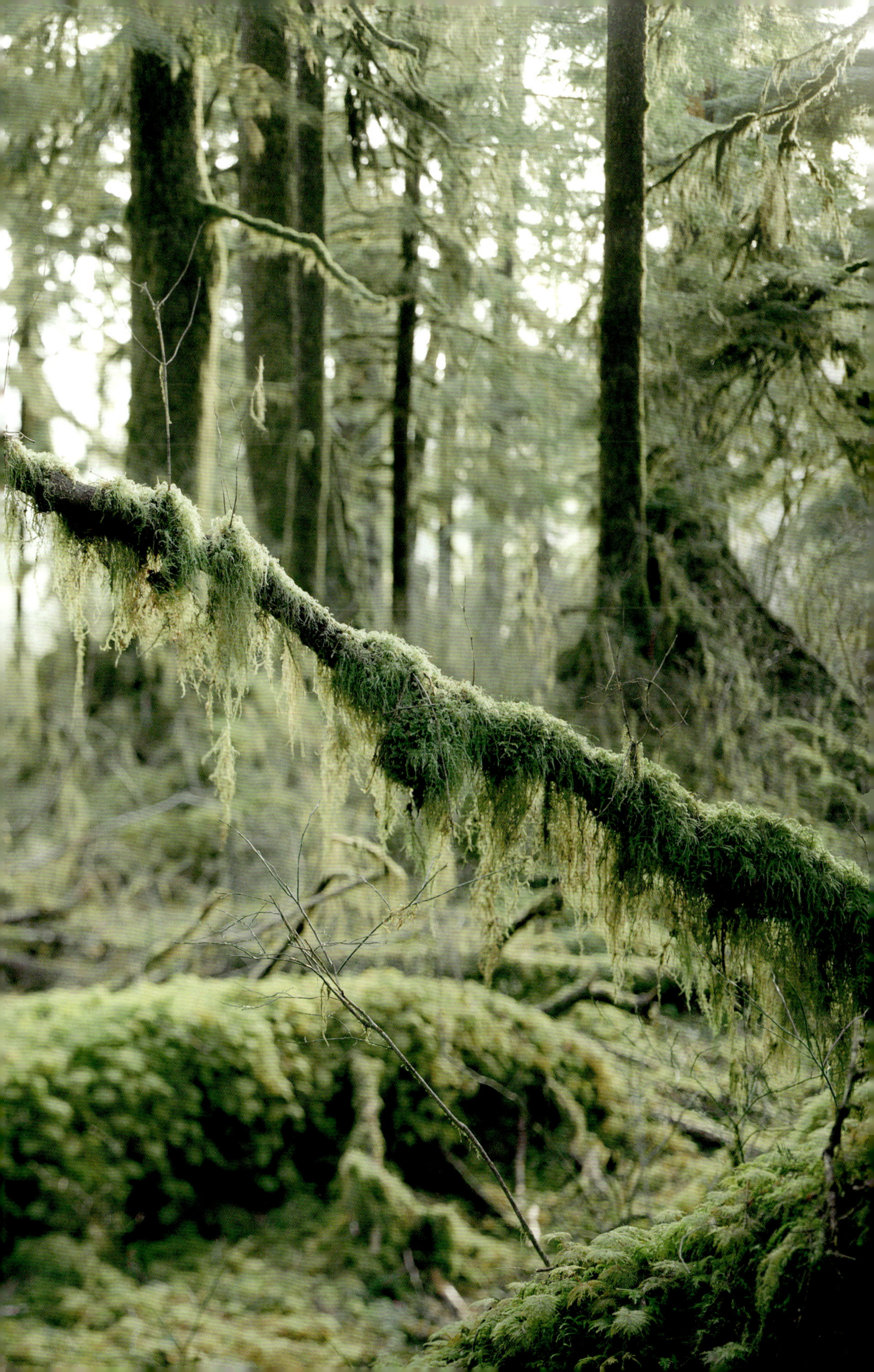

One of my six
brothers fell in love
with wood right from
the start. I remember
him handling and
fondling wood
even when he was
little. He spoke the
language of it. He
and wood liked each
other and got along
swell. He became a
forester and planted
trees, hundreds of
thousands of trees.
Do you know you
can plant a tree in
five seconds if you
get your stride right
and reach with one
hand and poke a
hole in the skin of
the earth and reach
up for the seedling
from your pack
with the other and
drop the seedling
and secure it in the
hole with your foot
as you continue on
apace? You can do
that. In some places
the woods are taking
over where farms
used to be. That
is happening in
Vermont and Maine.
When the woods
come back so do
animals that were
thought long gone,
like fisher and lion.

All the rest of his life my brother has worked with wood. He built houses and beds and chairs and tables and desks and cabinets and counters and lovely long curving tavern bars and pretty much anything else you can imagine you could persuade from wood. In his wood-shop there are chunks of twenty kinds of wood.

One time I asked him what he was going to do with a particularly weighty chunk and he said he was waiting for the wood to tell him what it wanted to be. I think about that remark a lot and always come away refreshed by the respect and humility in it. More and more these days I think humility is the final frontier. We spend many years building ego and then if we are lucky we realize we need to cut it down and saw it up and turn it into something shy.

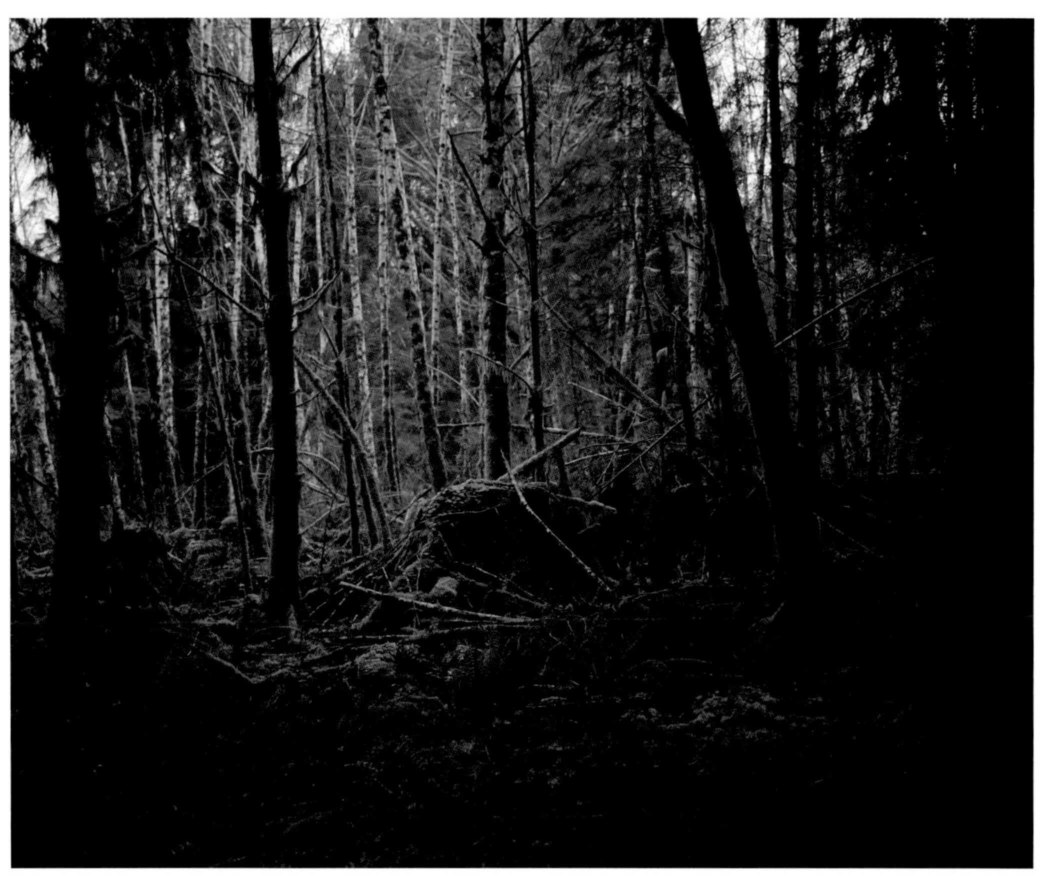

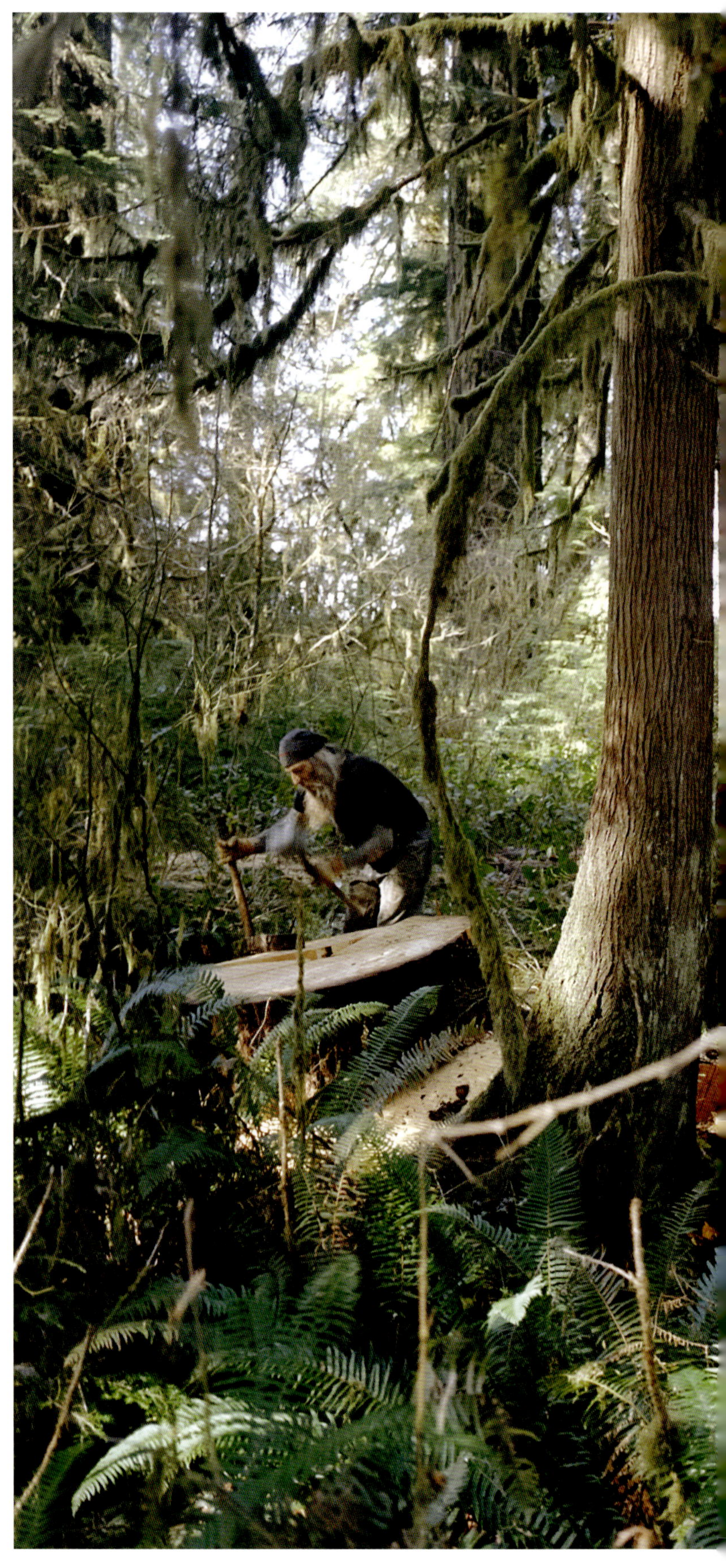

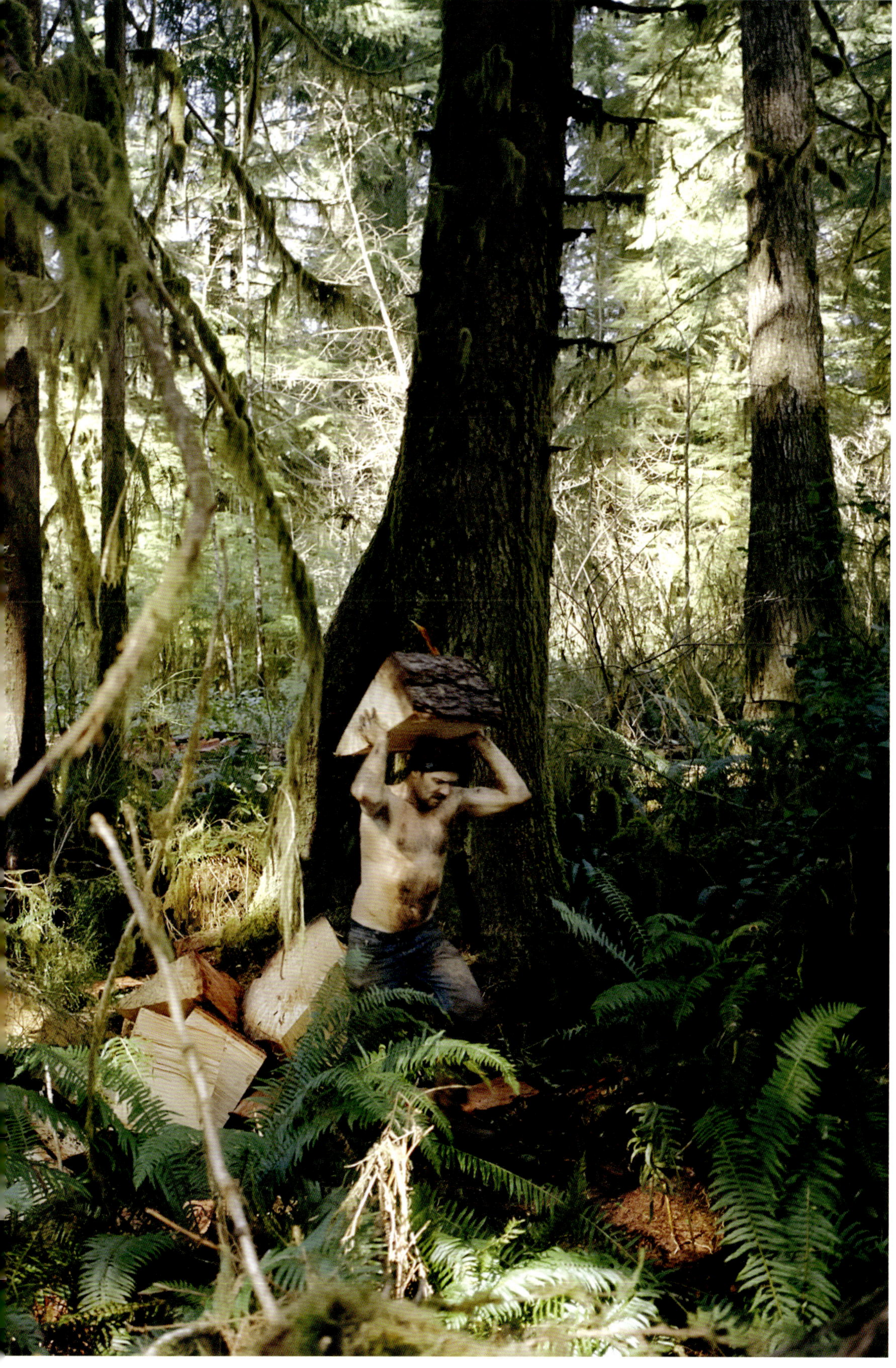

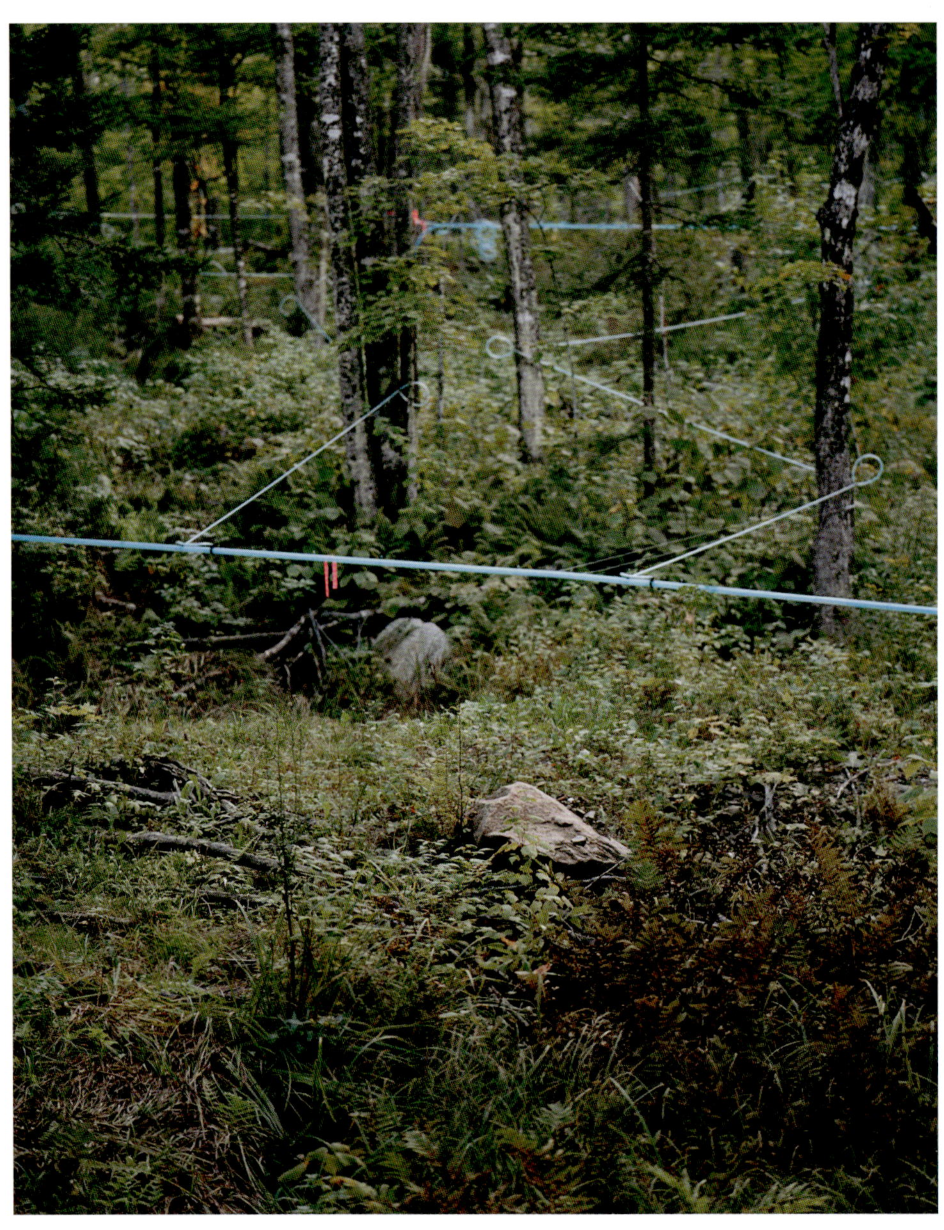

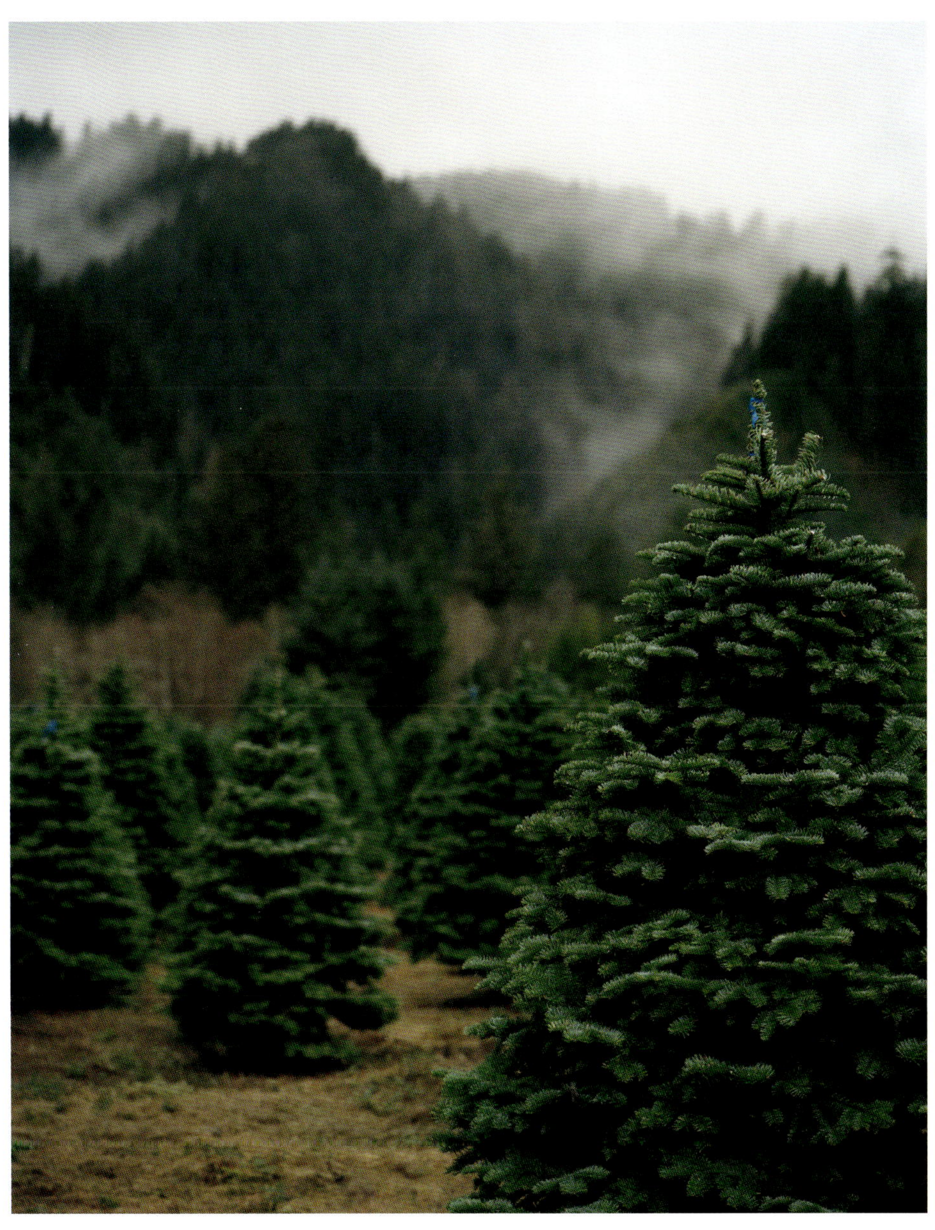

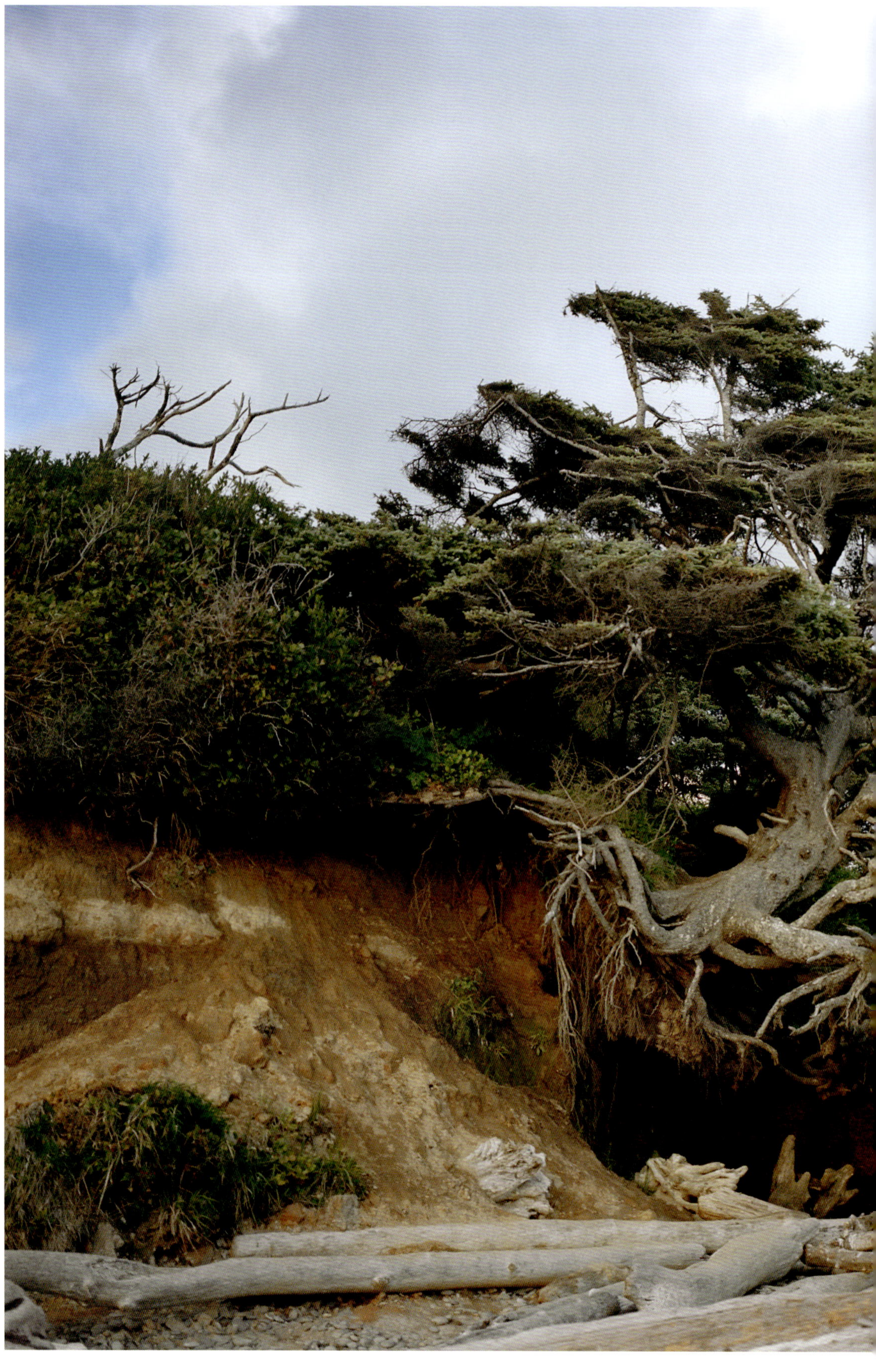

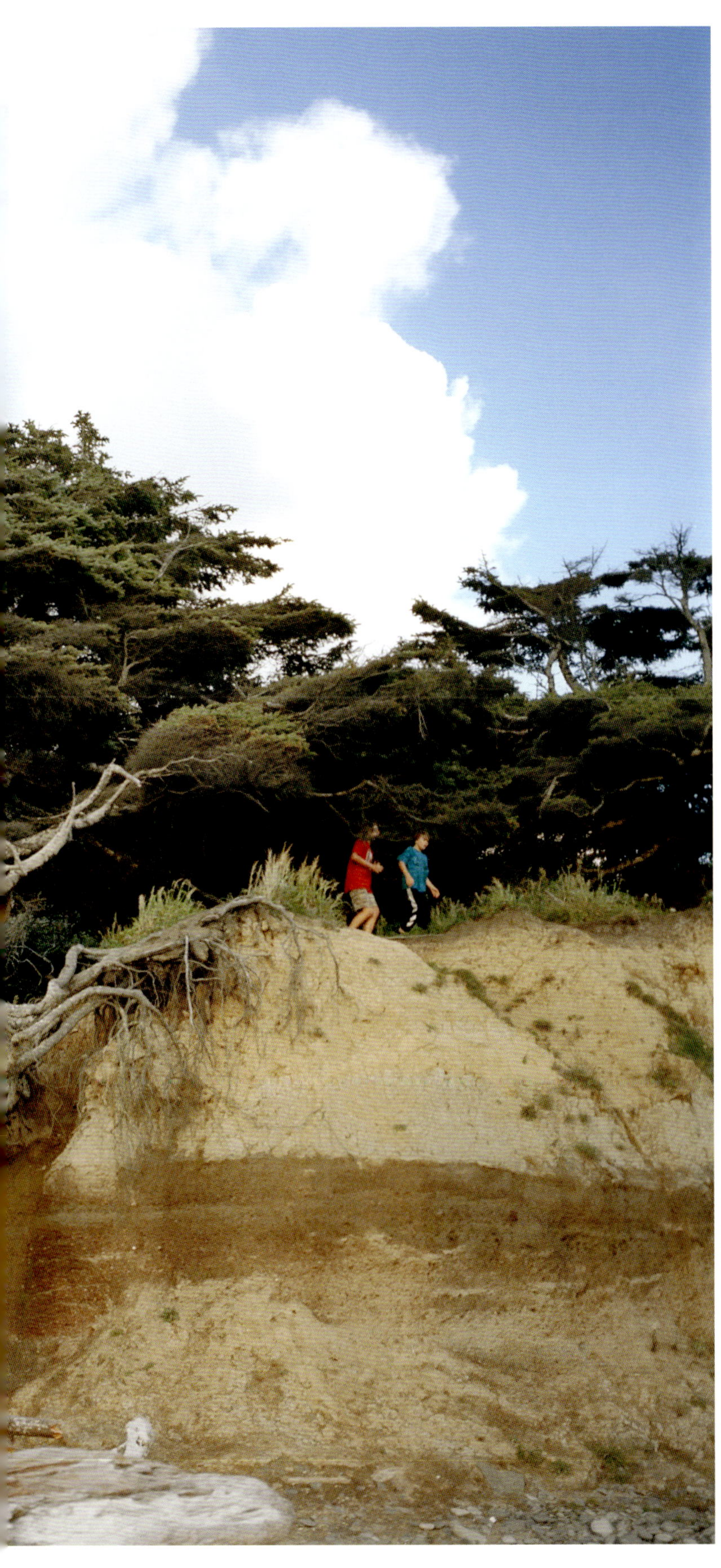

Q: Do trees think and feel?

A: Of course not, not in any way that we know the words think and feel. But that's the point, isn't it? I suggest that they consider and ponder and absorb and apprehend the world in very different ways than we do, and we do not quite understand the verb of their lives. We think of them as nouns, stationary, serene, placid, substantive, stolid, stern; but imagine if you could absorb nutrition from the very earth with your intricate spidery toes. Imagine that you could eat light and sip clouds. Imagine if you too lived to be five thousand years old, like bristlecone pines, or were four hundred feet tall, like redwoods, or weighed a thousand tons, like sequoias, or spent your life on a ridge above the lithe Wilson River as it made its way toward mother Ocean. How does the tree perceive the river? Like an ouzel that never stops singing? How does the tree consider its companions? Do their roots tangle and tease? What do they feel? Because we cannot understand how they could feel, does that mean that they do not feel? If you do not know a thing, does that mean the thing is impossible? No? Well, then…

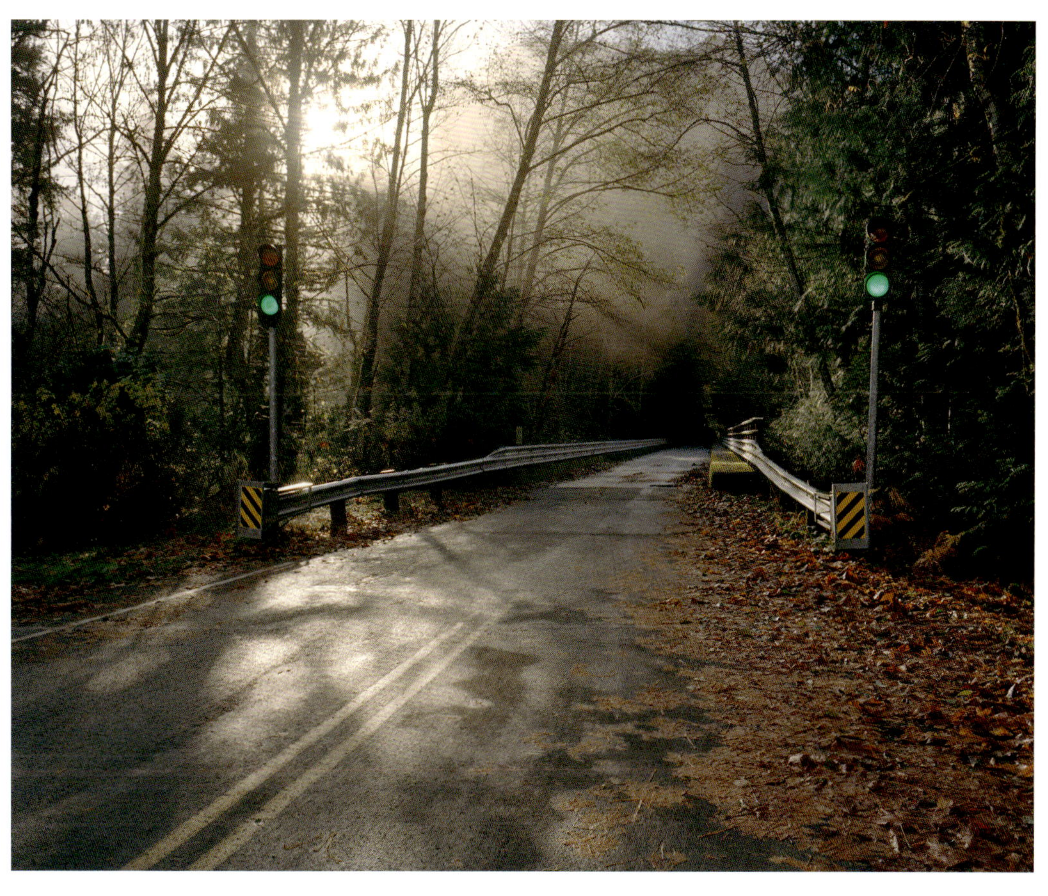

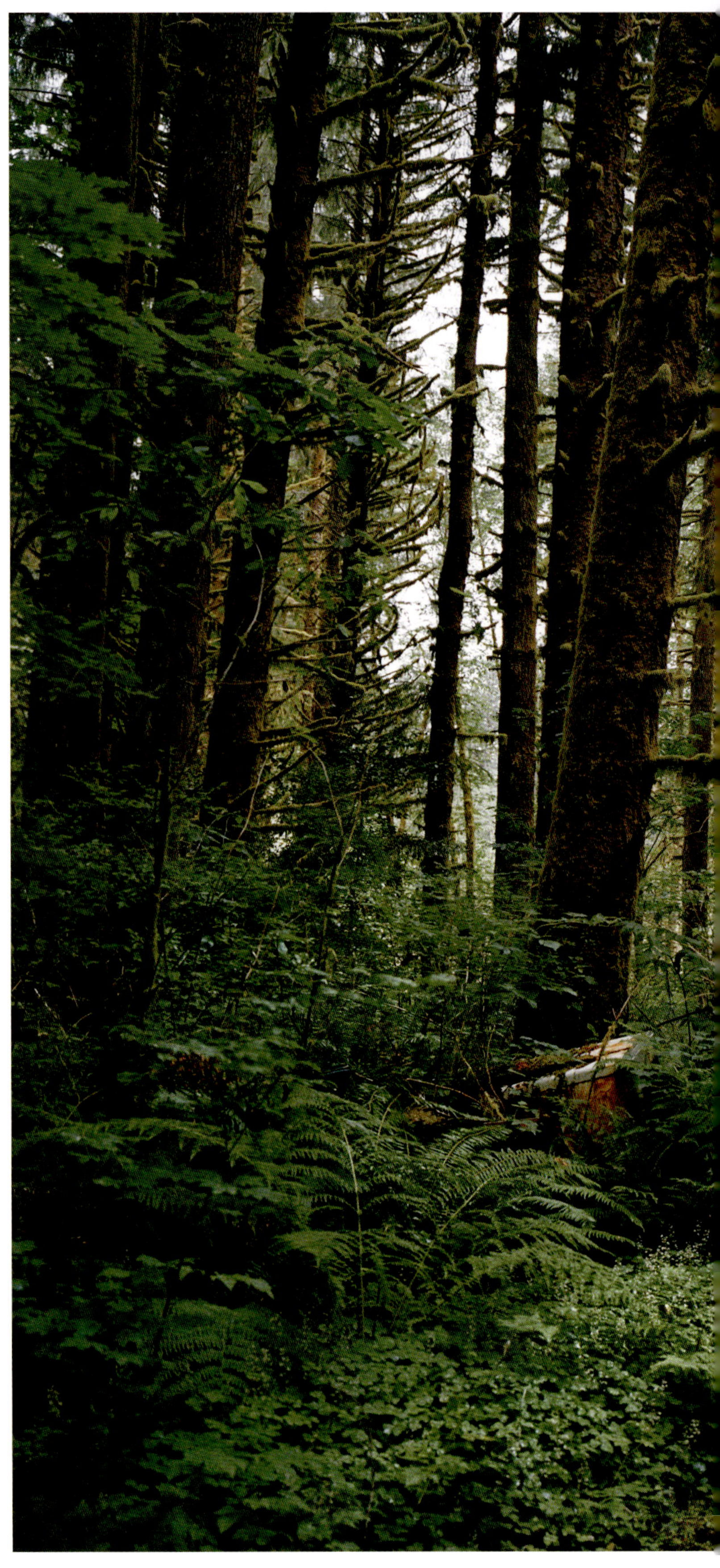

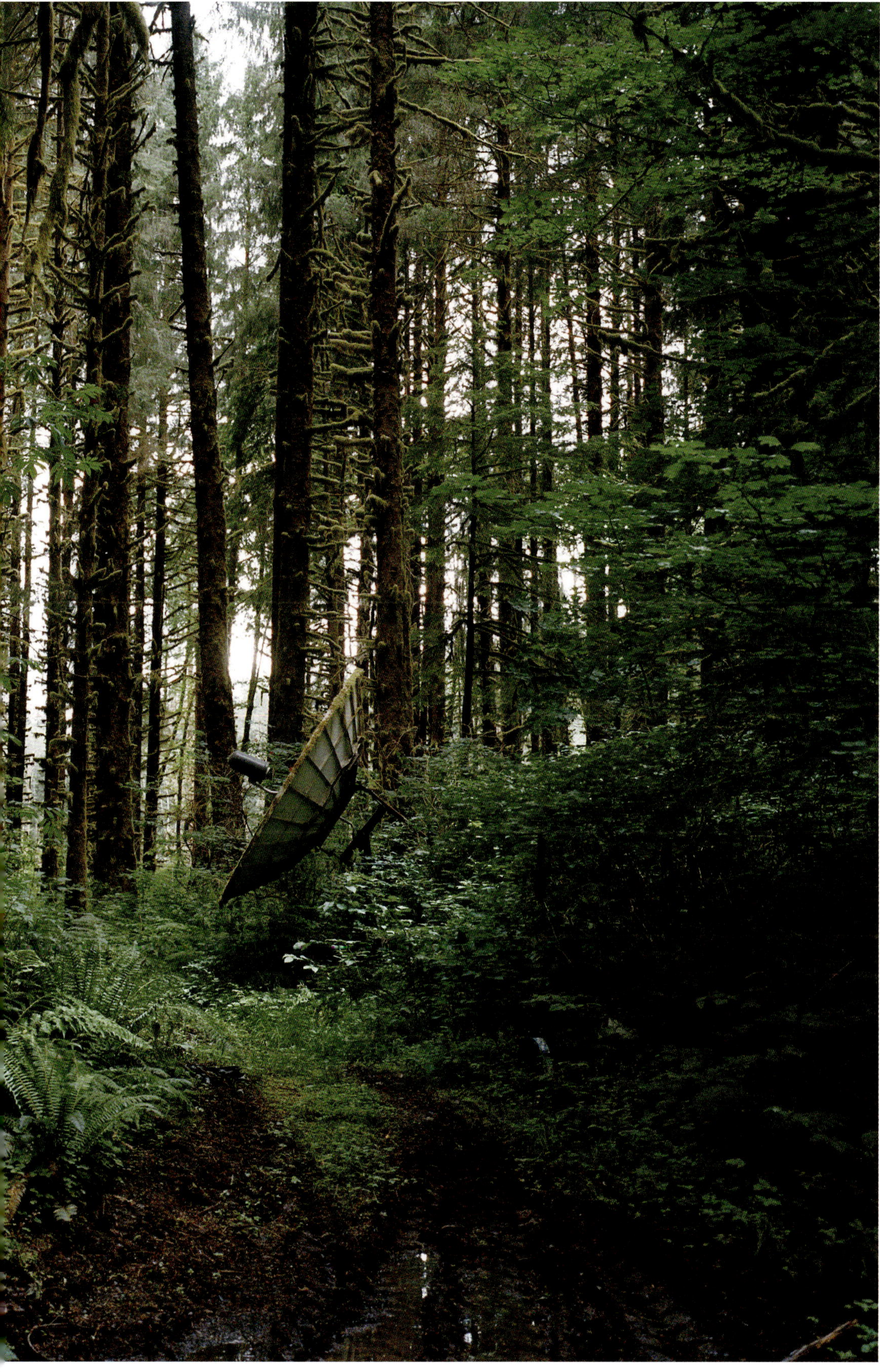

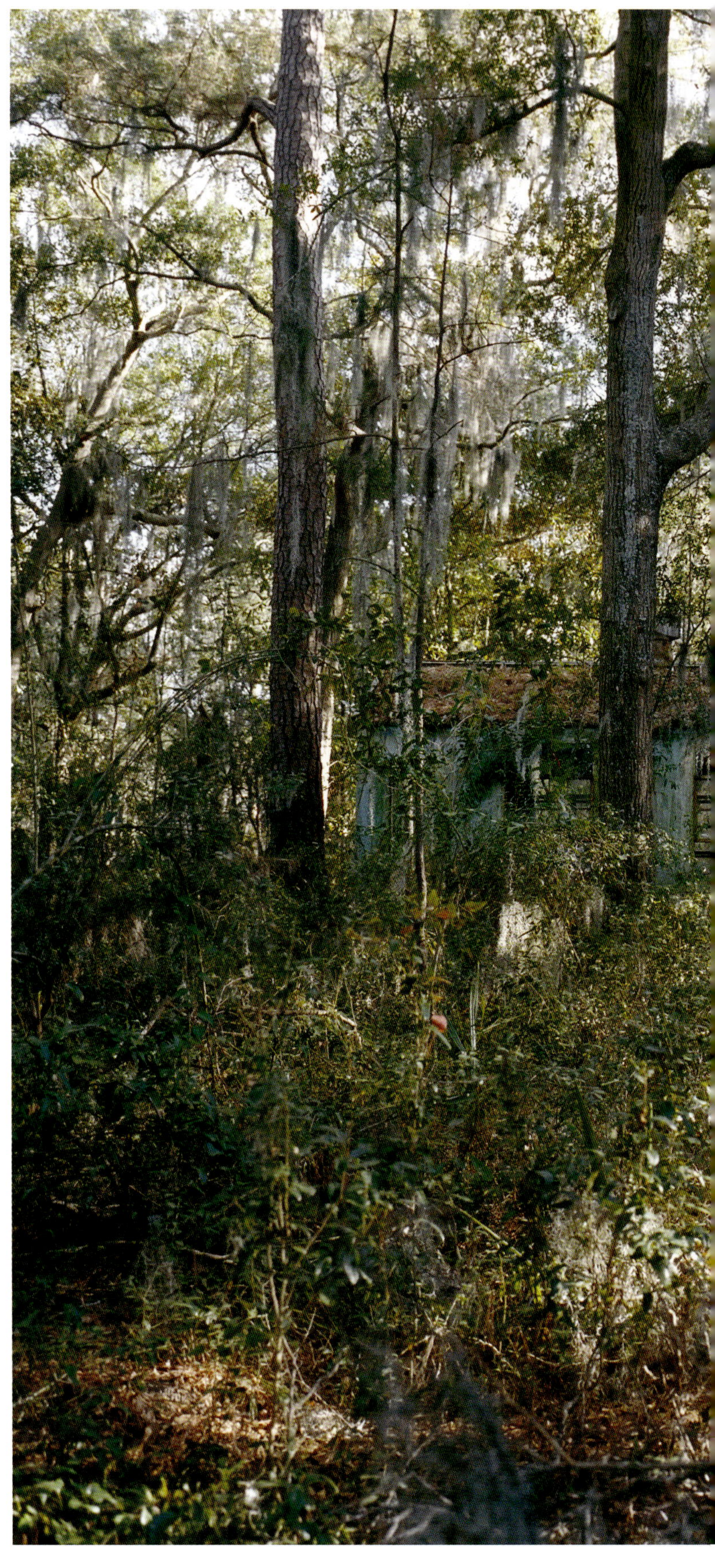

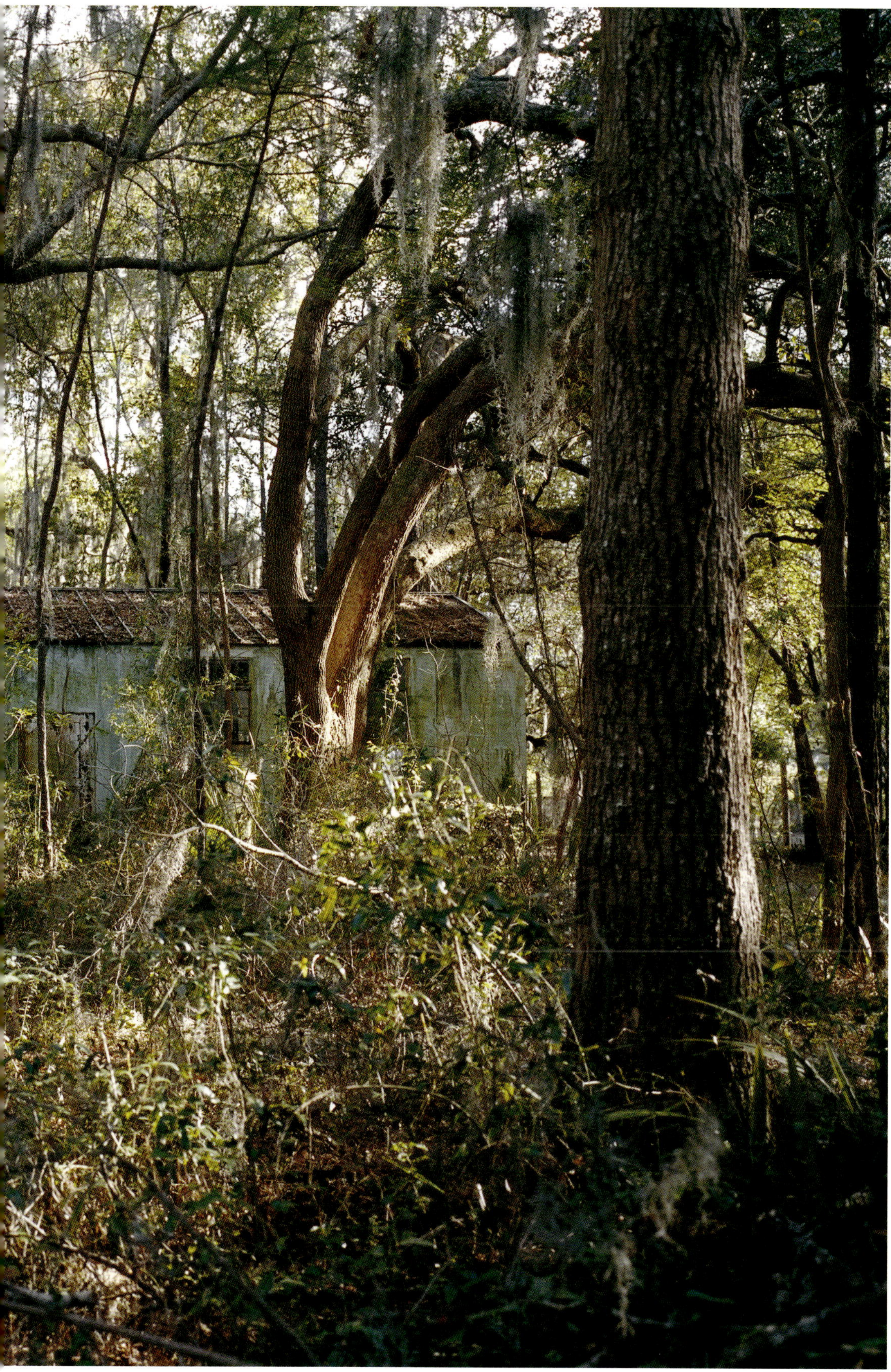

When I was a little kid
I thought that lakes
were like huge blue and
green and brown eyes in
the forest, and once in

a while, even now, all
these years later, when
I achieve childishness
again, fitfully and
delightedly – I still do.

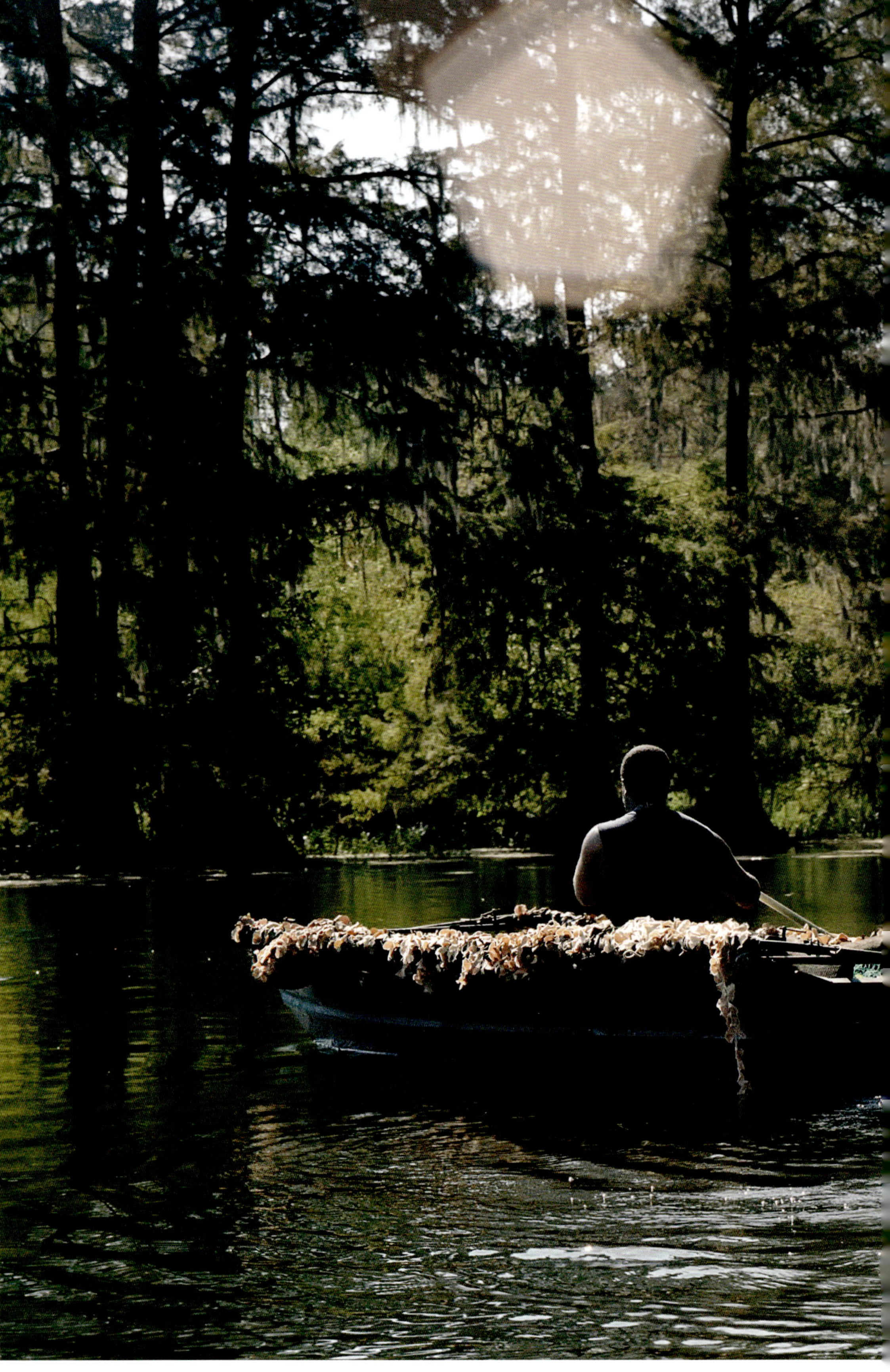

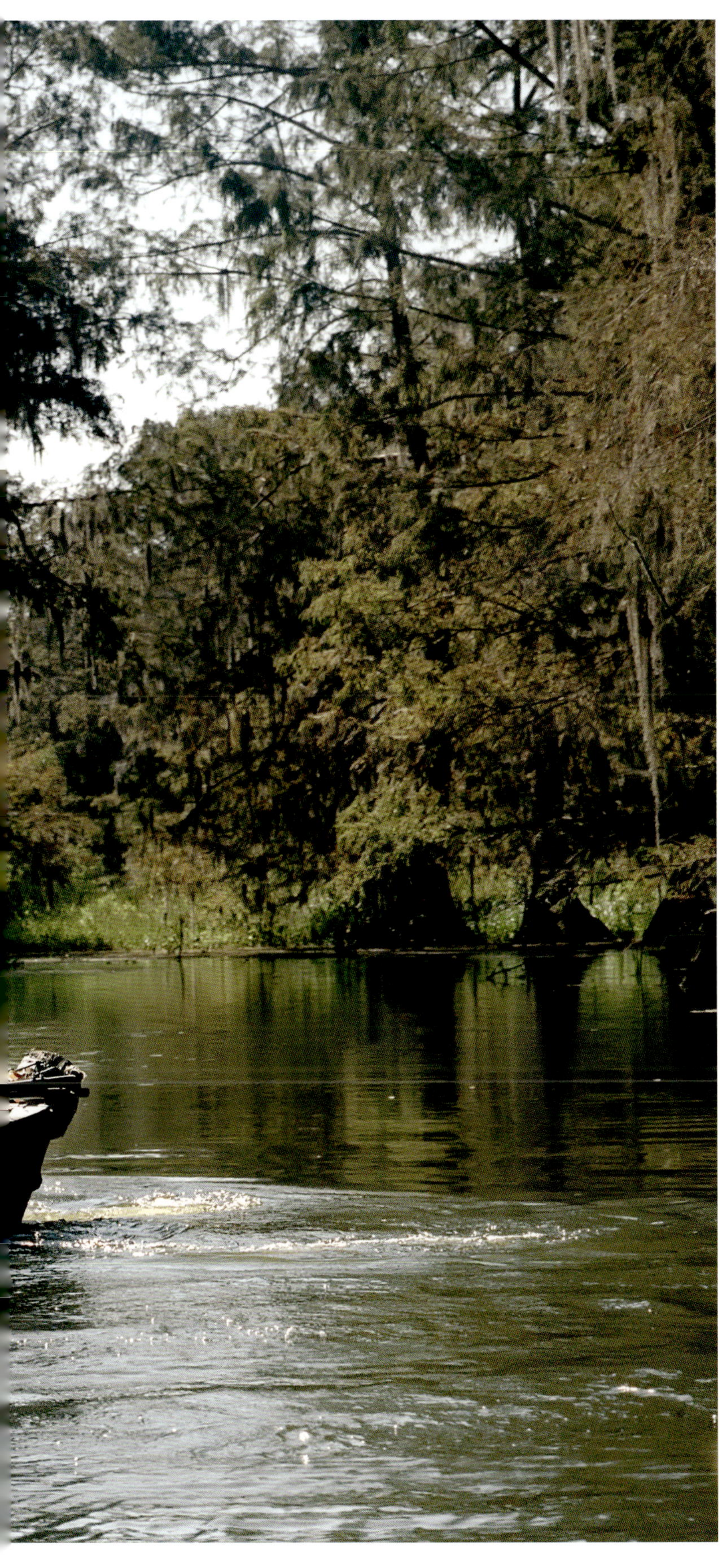

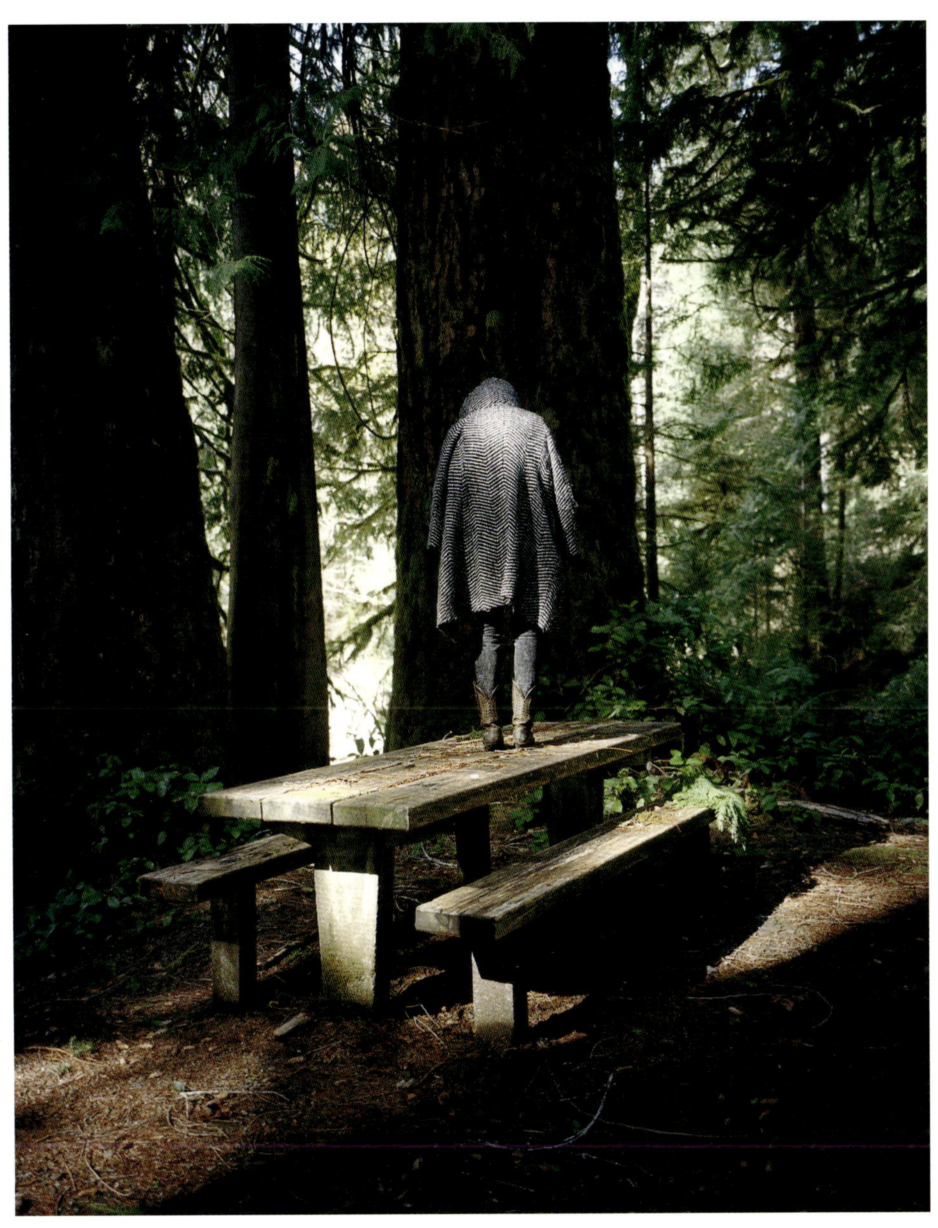

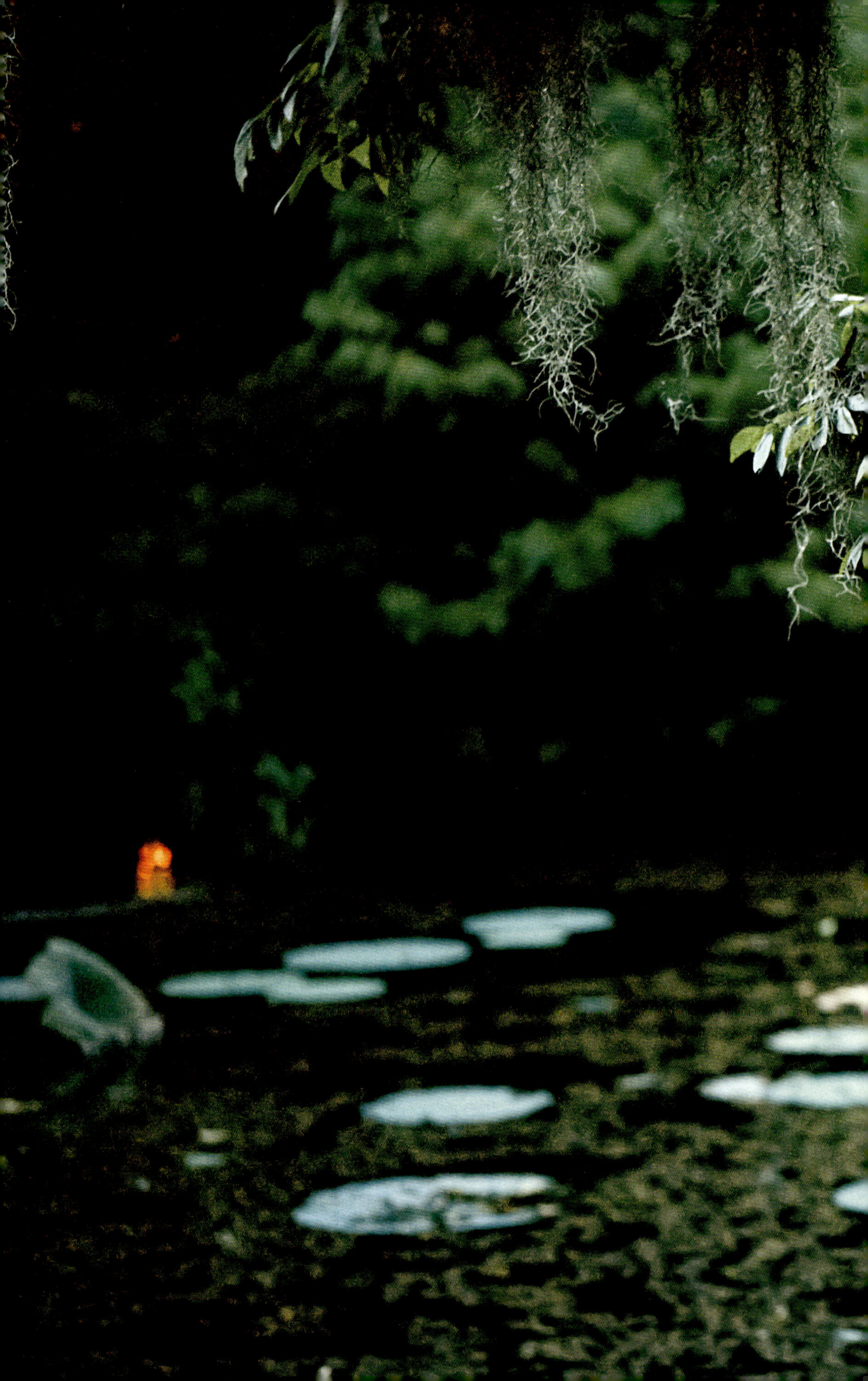

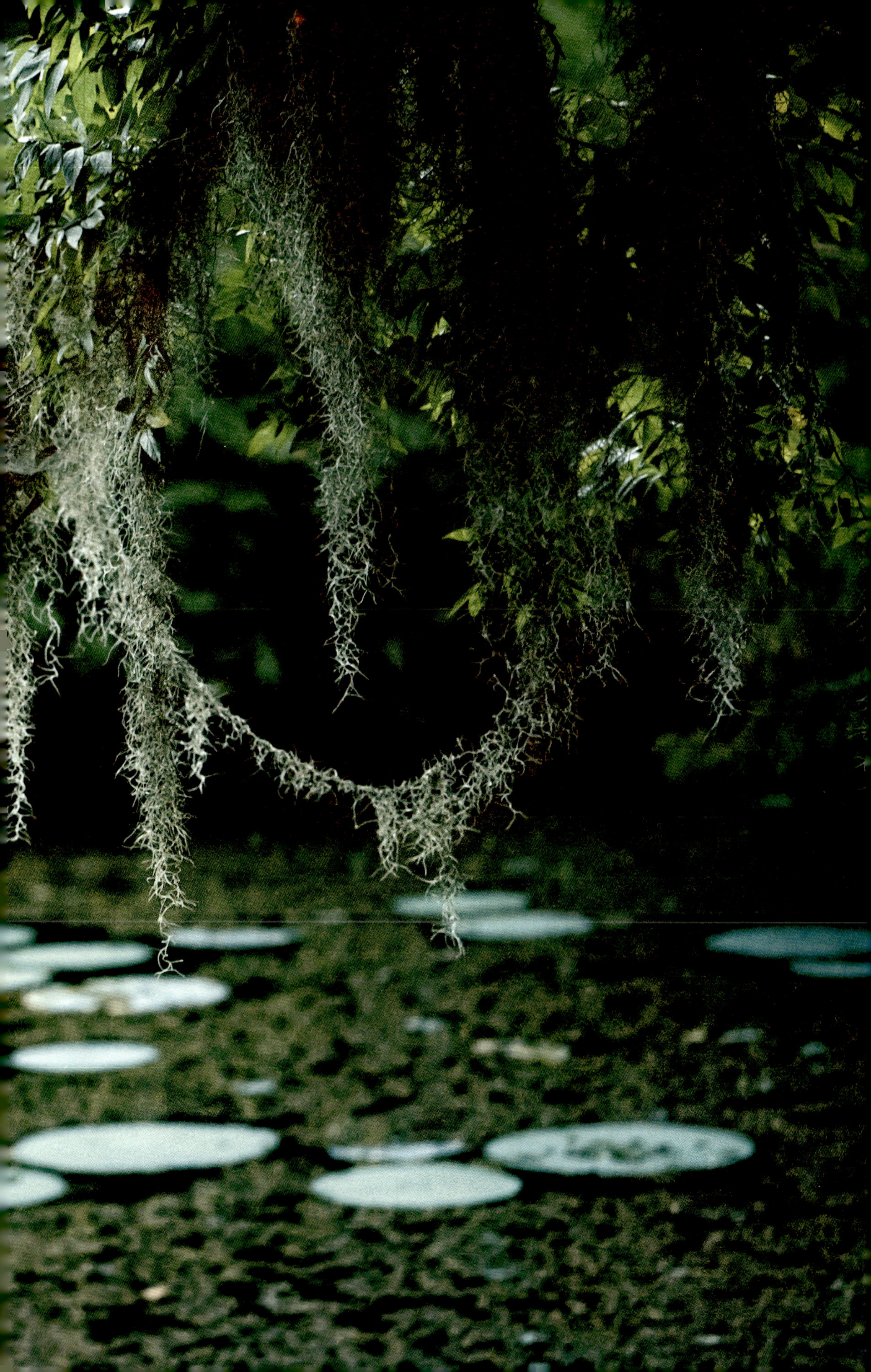

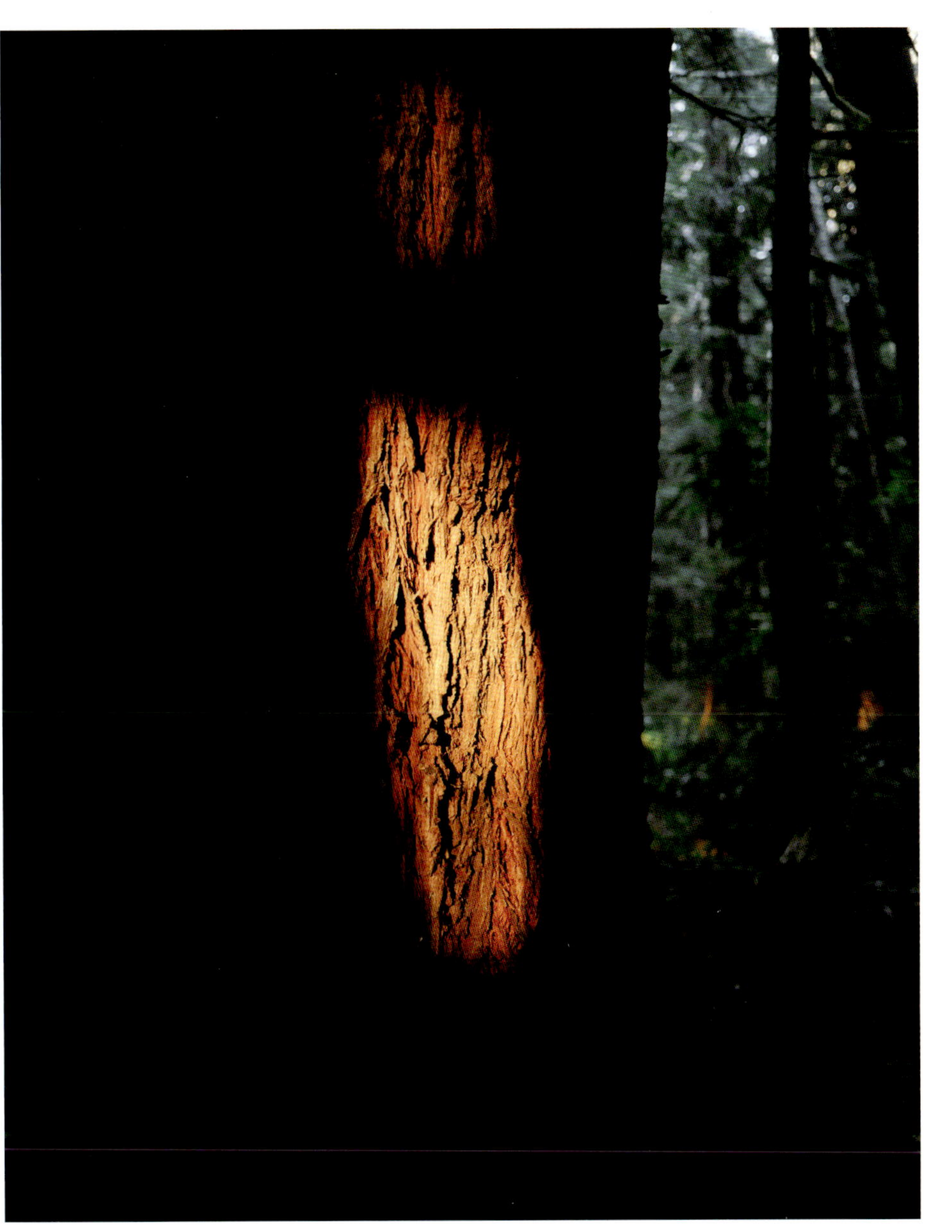

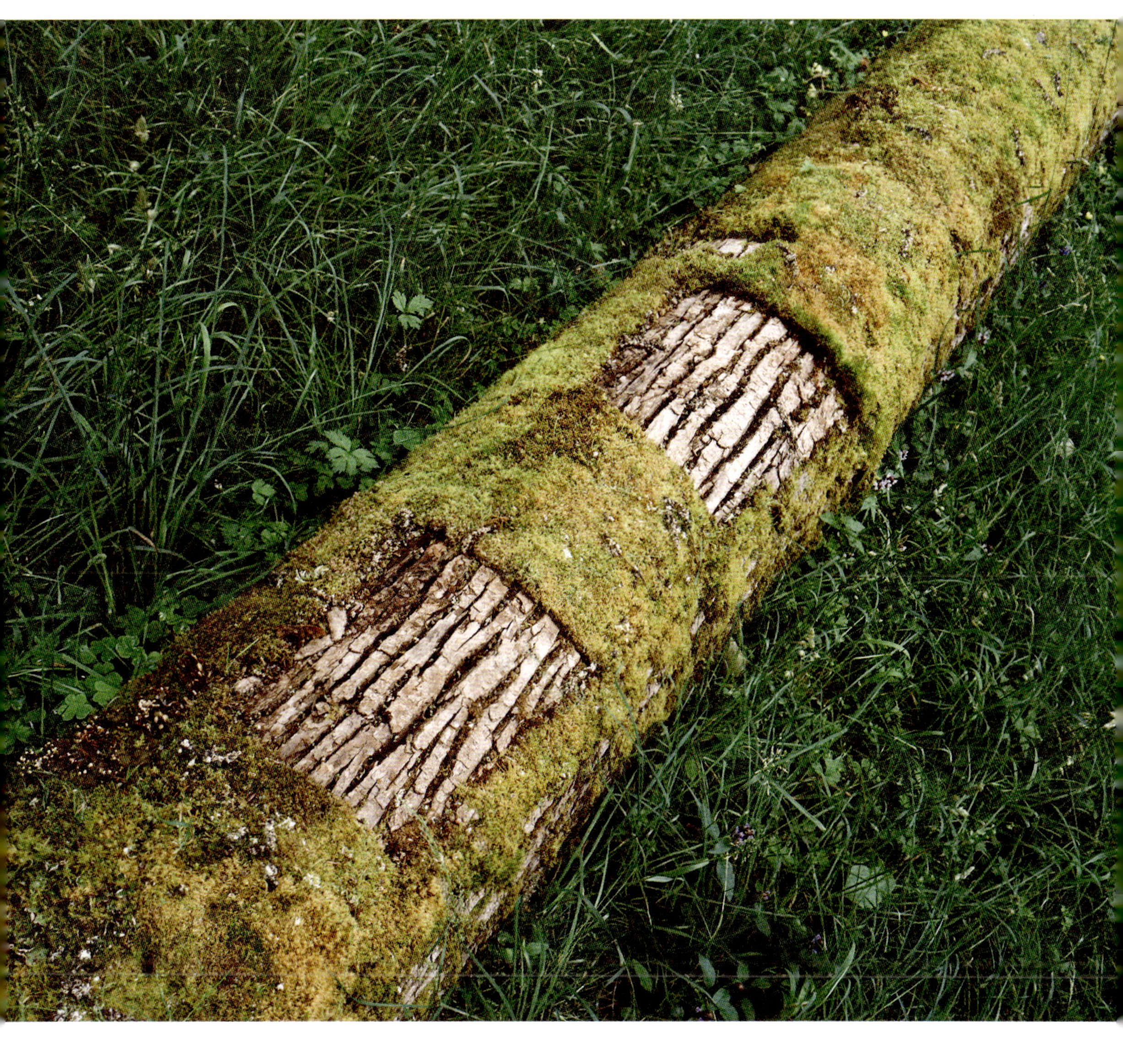

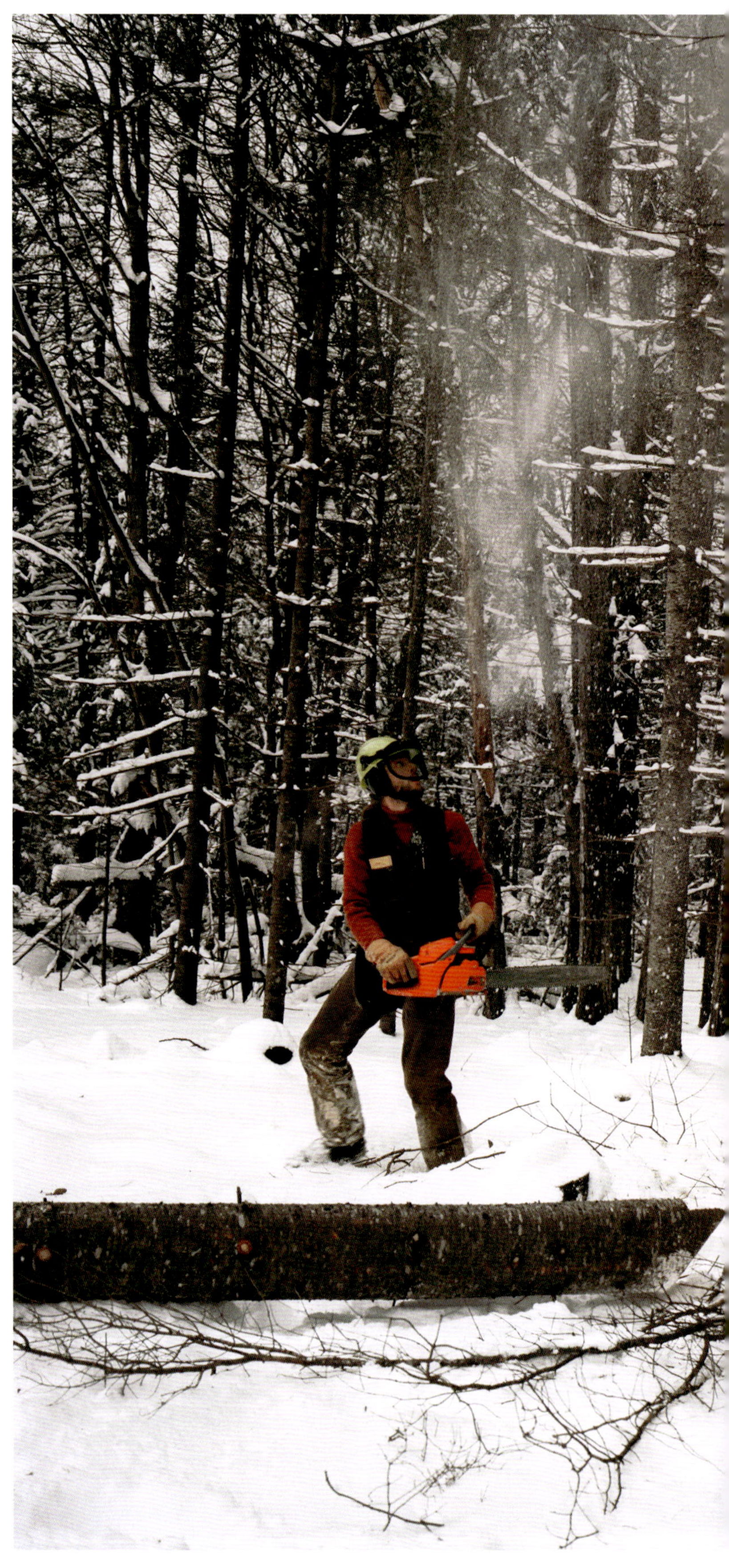

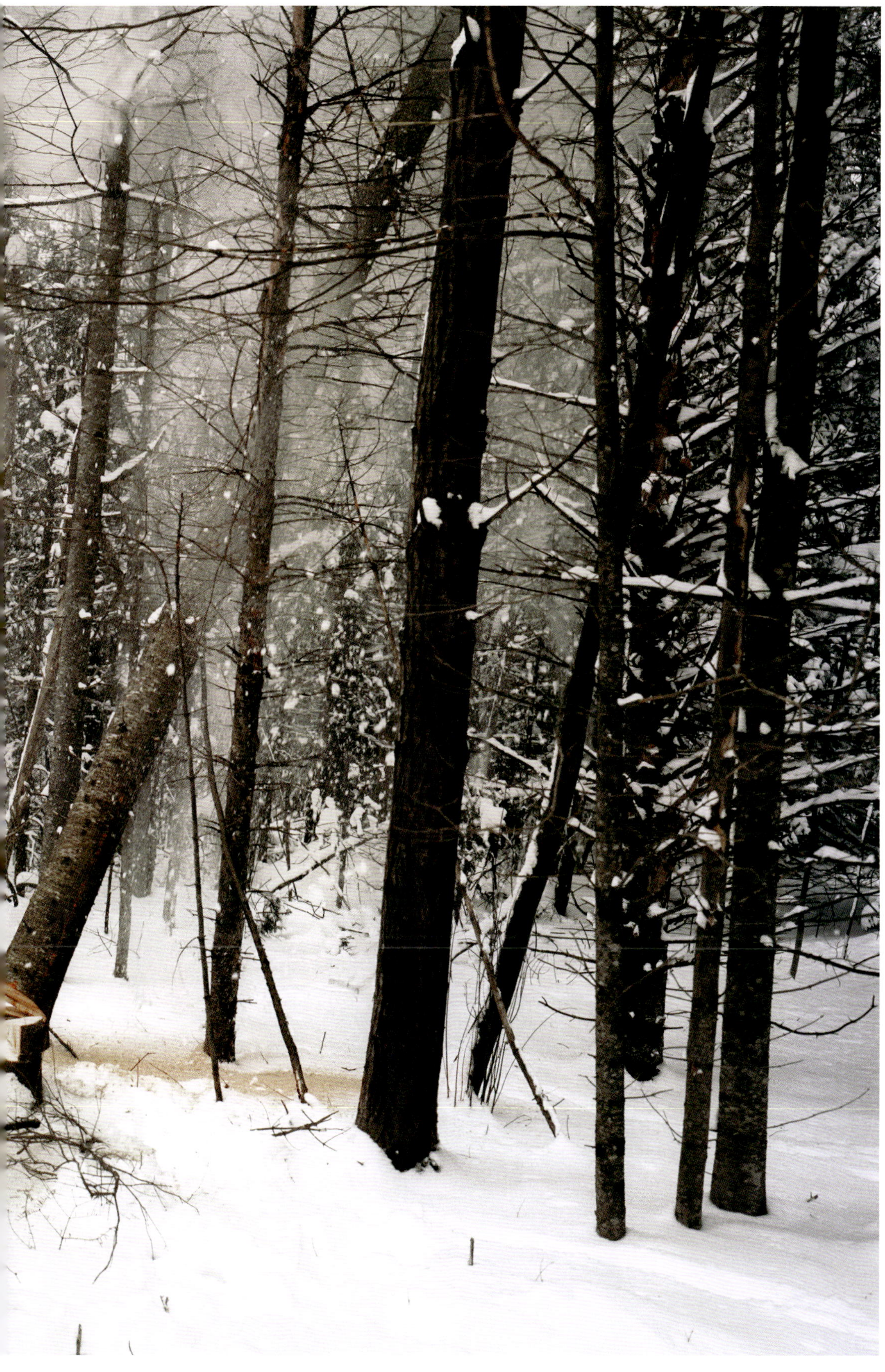

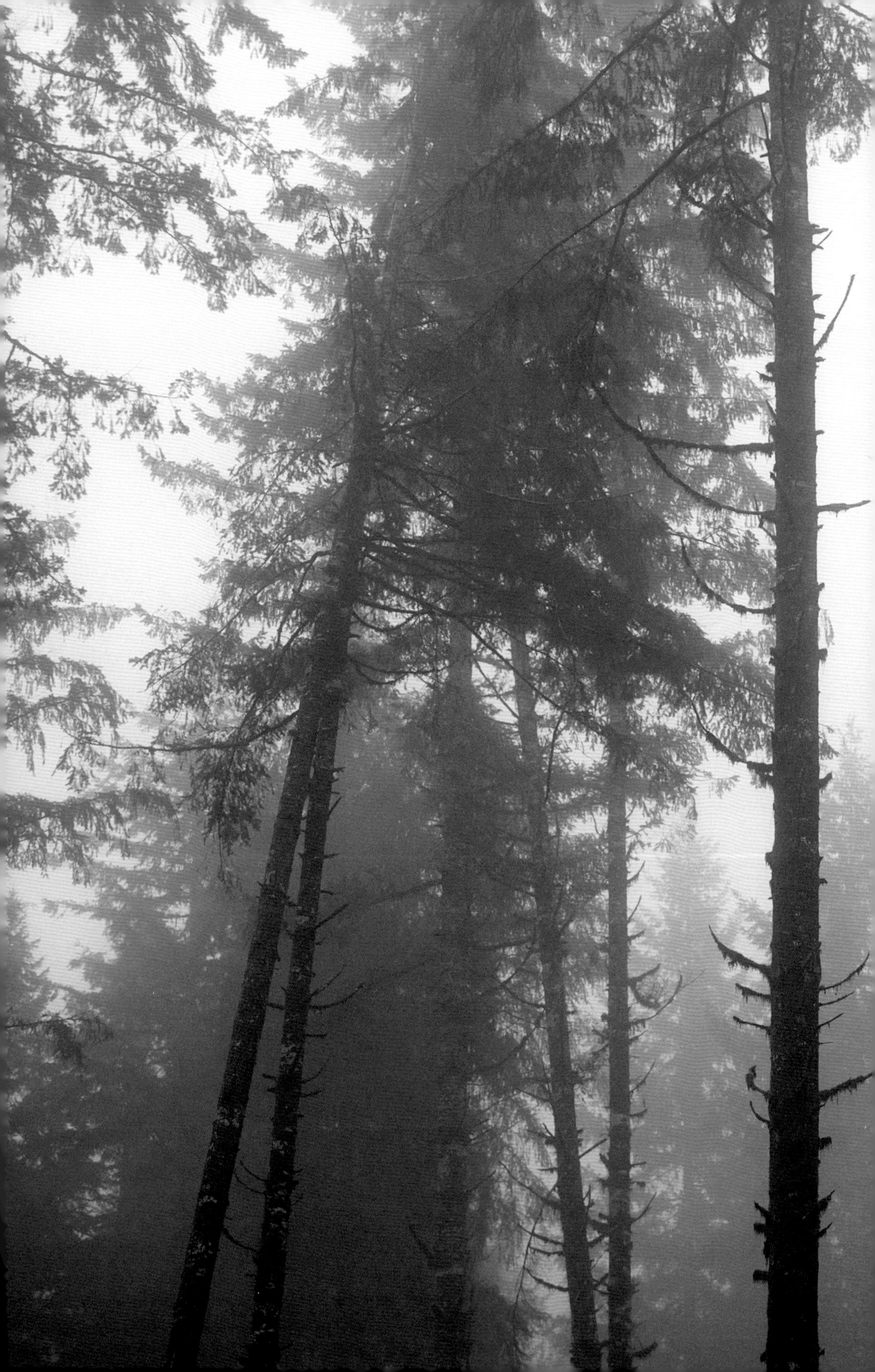

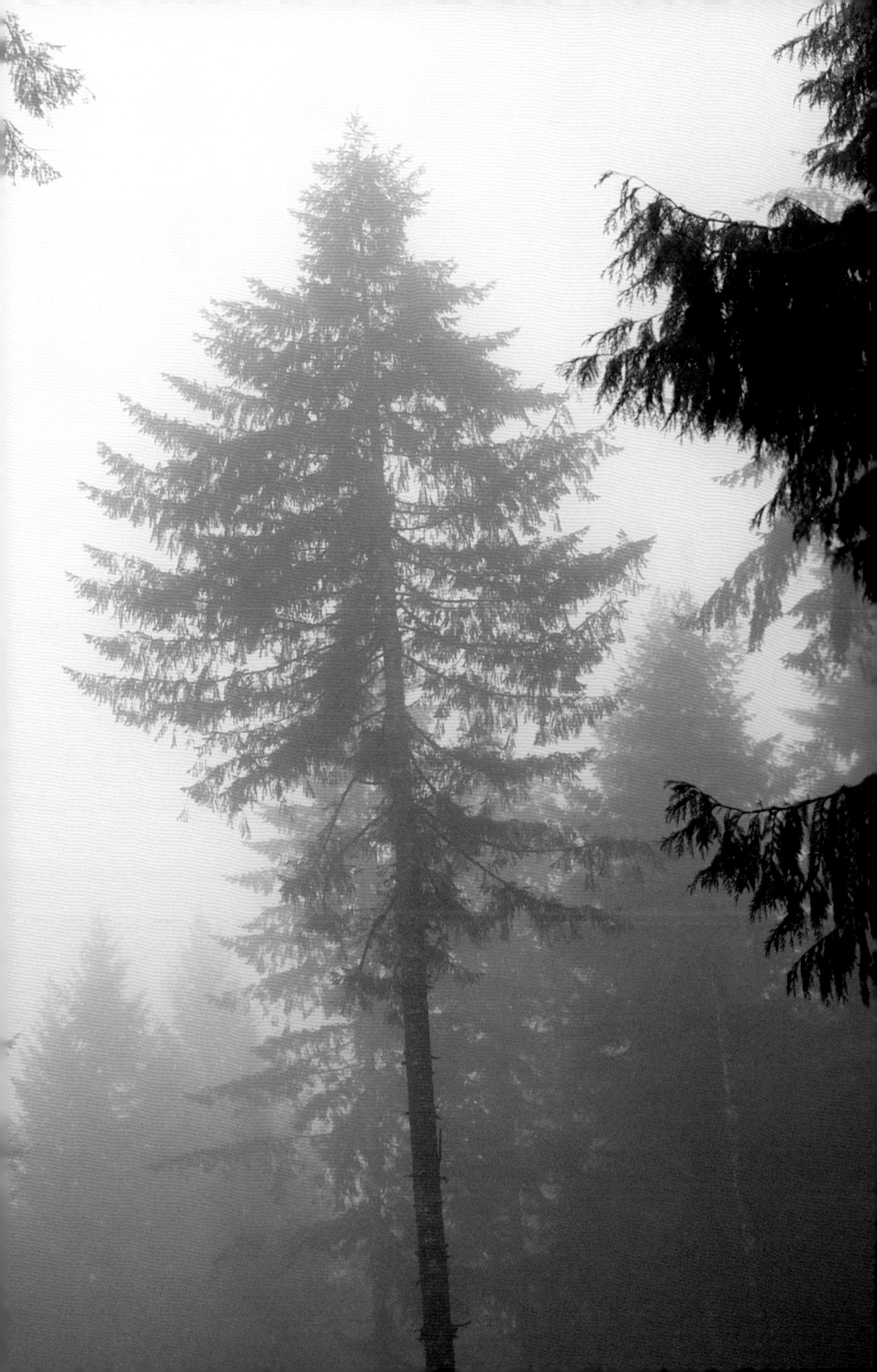

No one more admires what it is we do with wood. We build schools and chapels and churches and houses and homes and cabins and sheds and bridges and roads and trails and paths and desks and bars and barrels and buckets and shingles and shakes and boxes and rinks and frames and steps and stairs and crosses and crucifixes and boats and ships and carts and wagons and hoops and bows and arrows and roofs and bins and shims and coffins and I could continue this sentence for a week. But probably you are like me, and every once in a while, when you see a pile of logs, they look awfully like corpses, don't they? Just for an instant? And so they are.

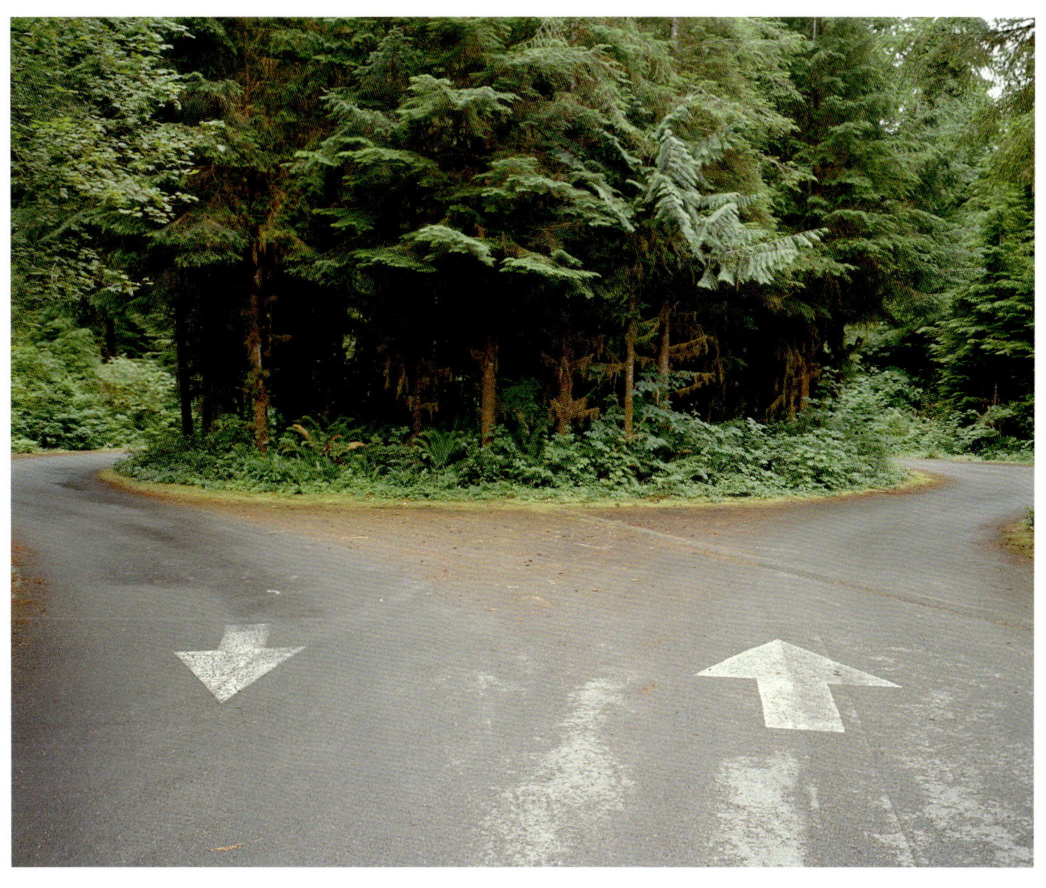

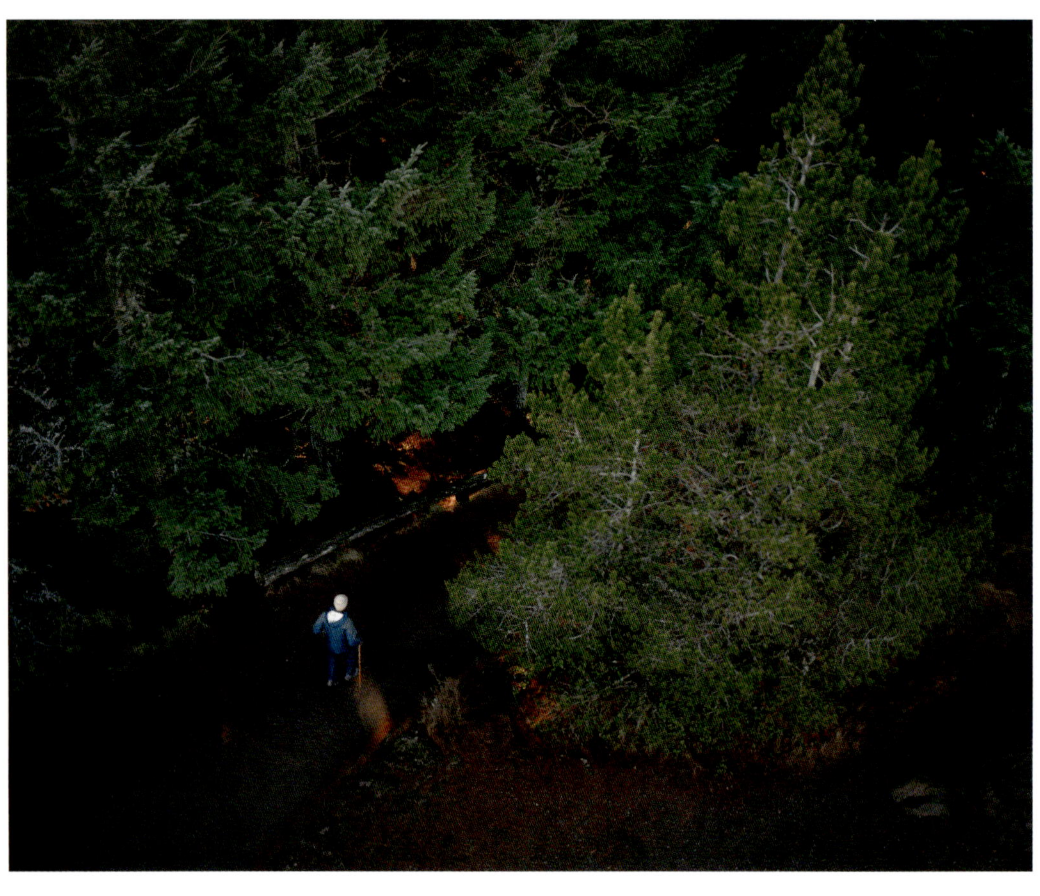

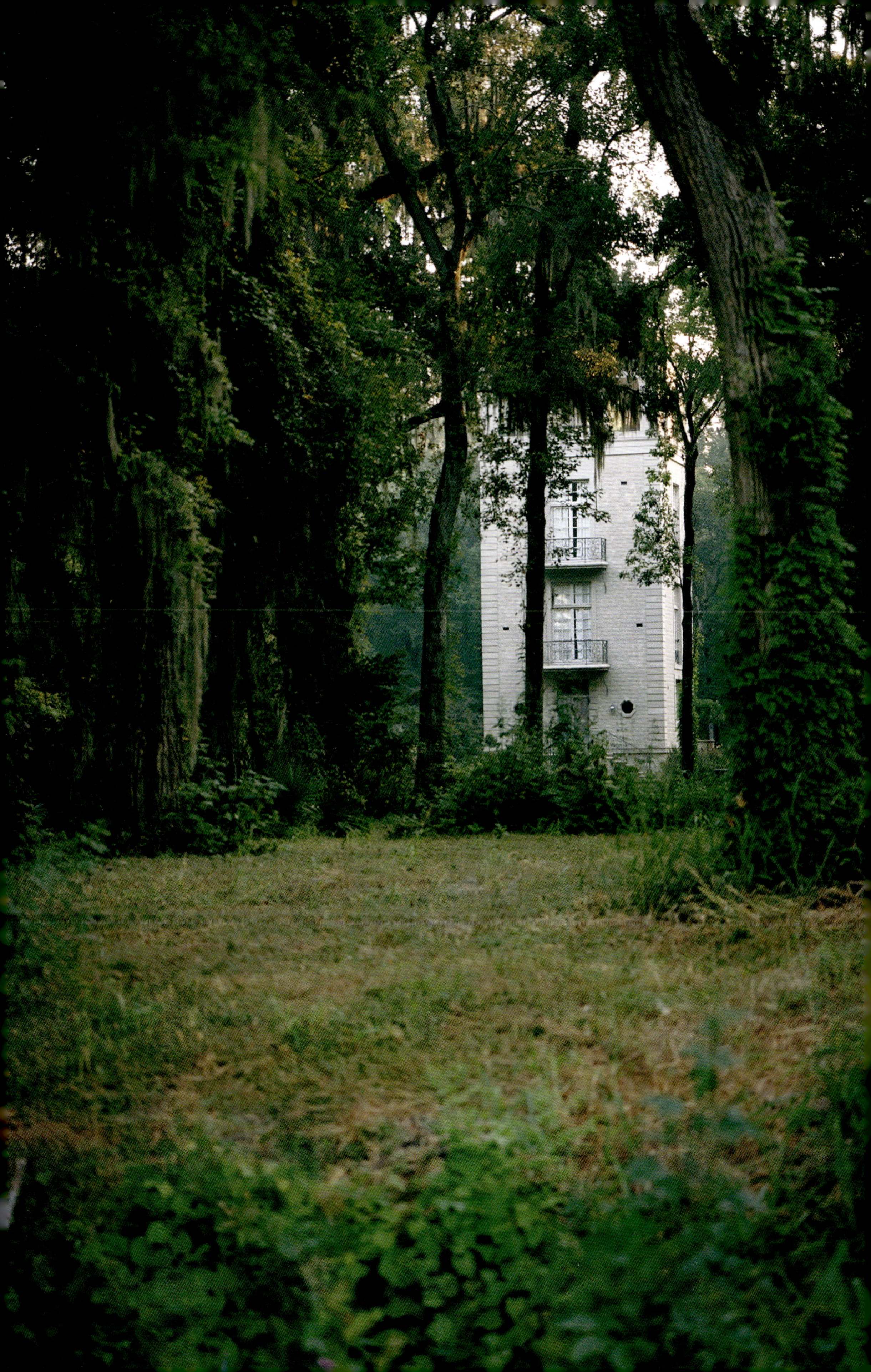

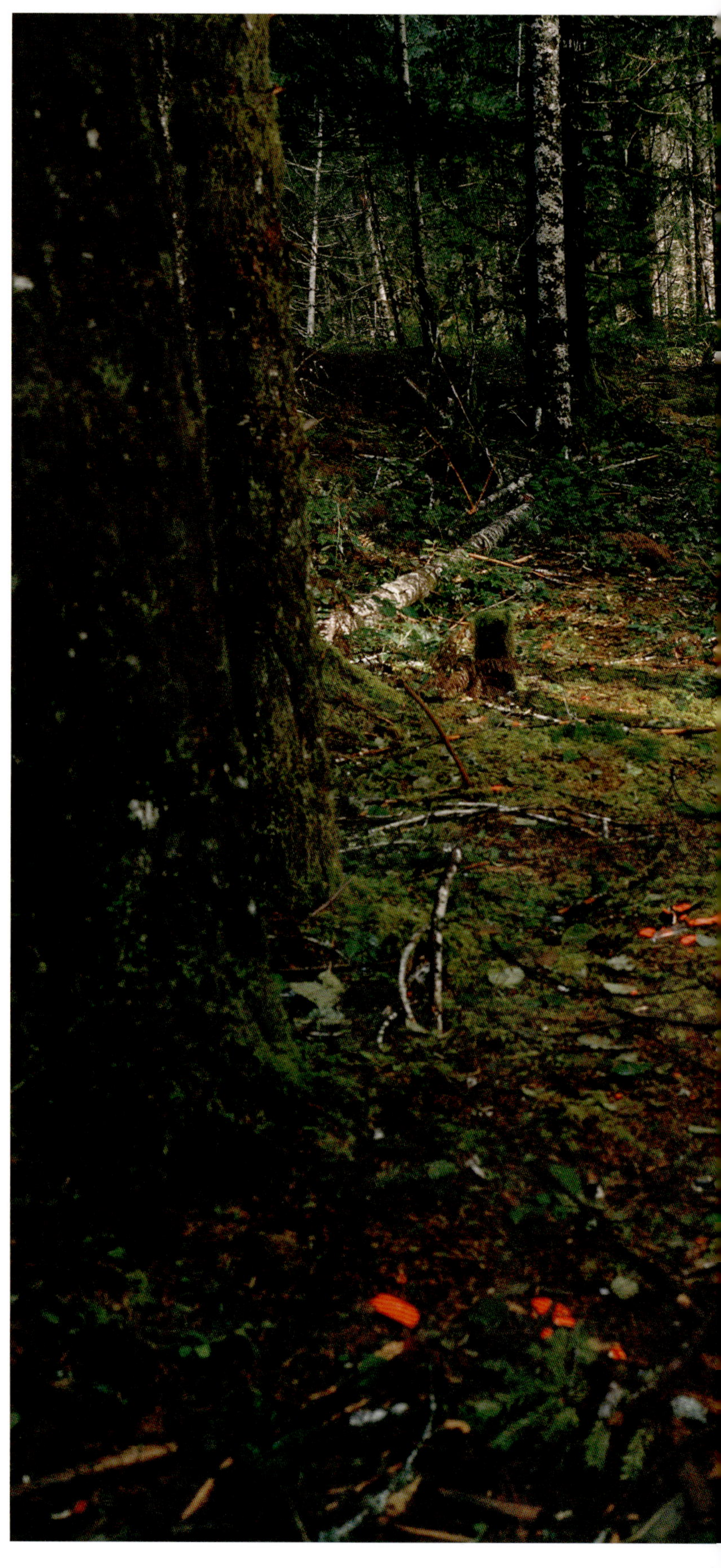

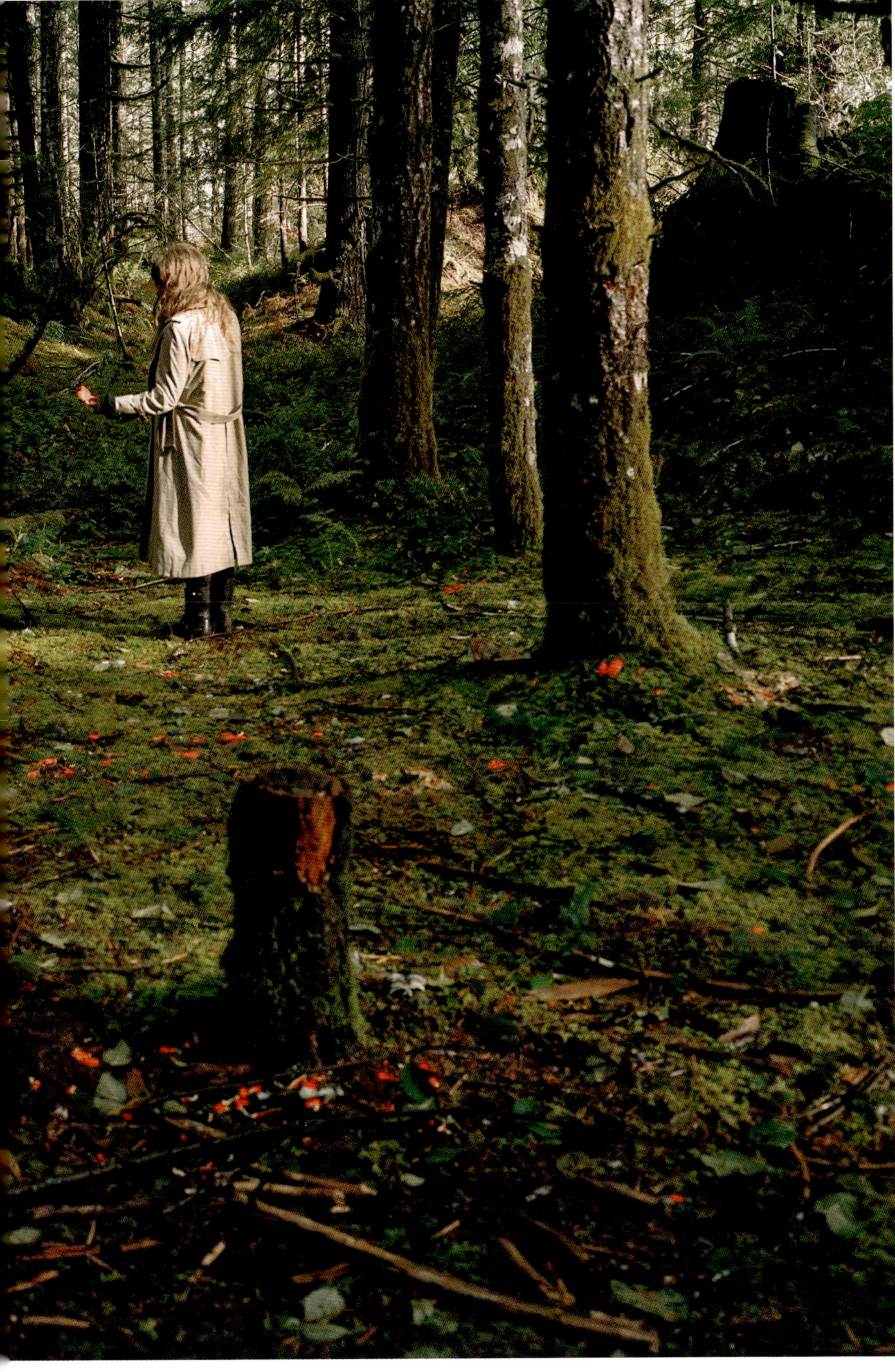

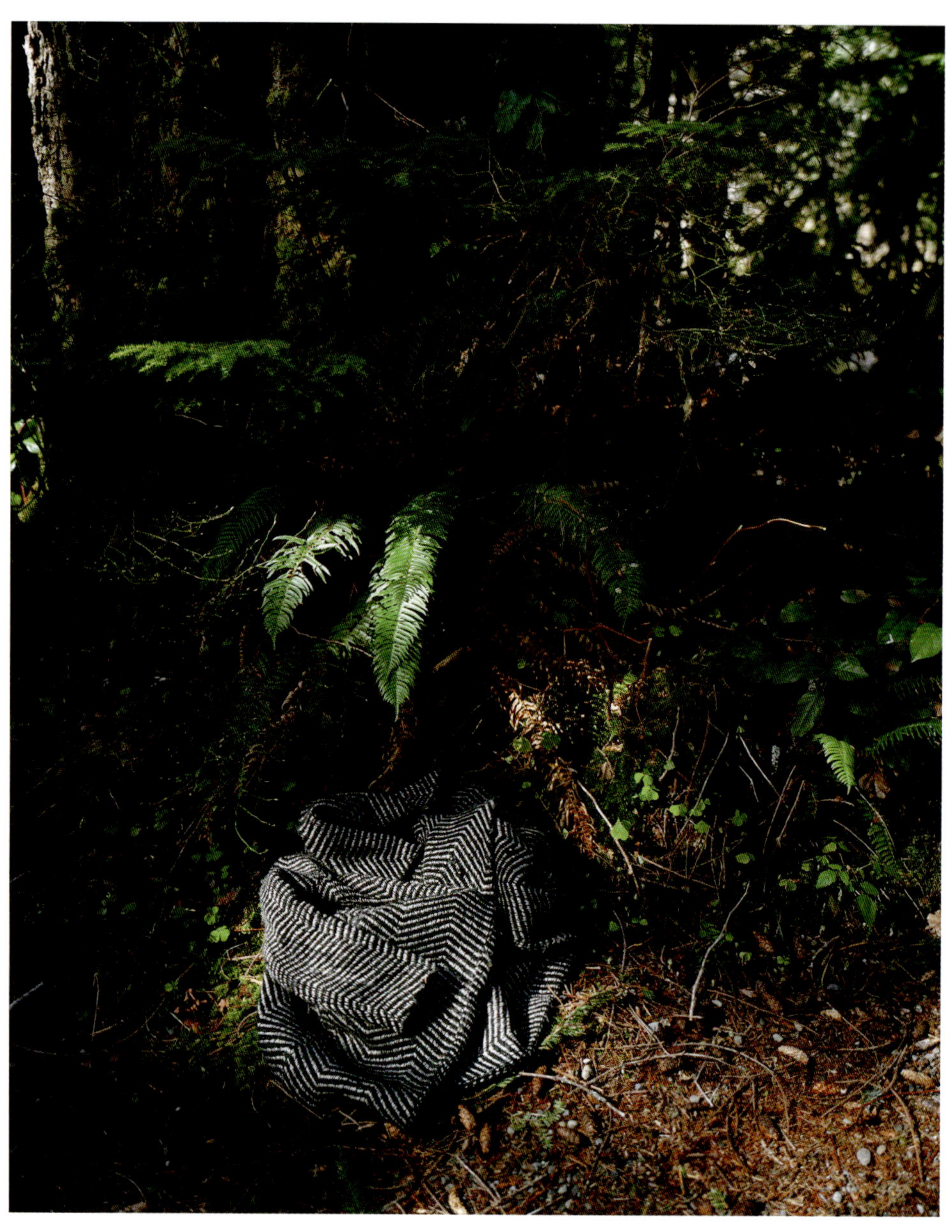

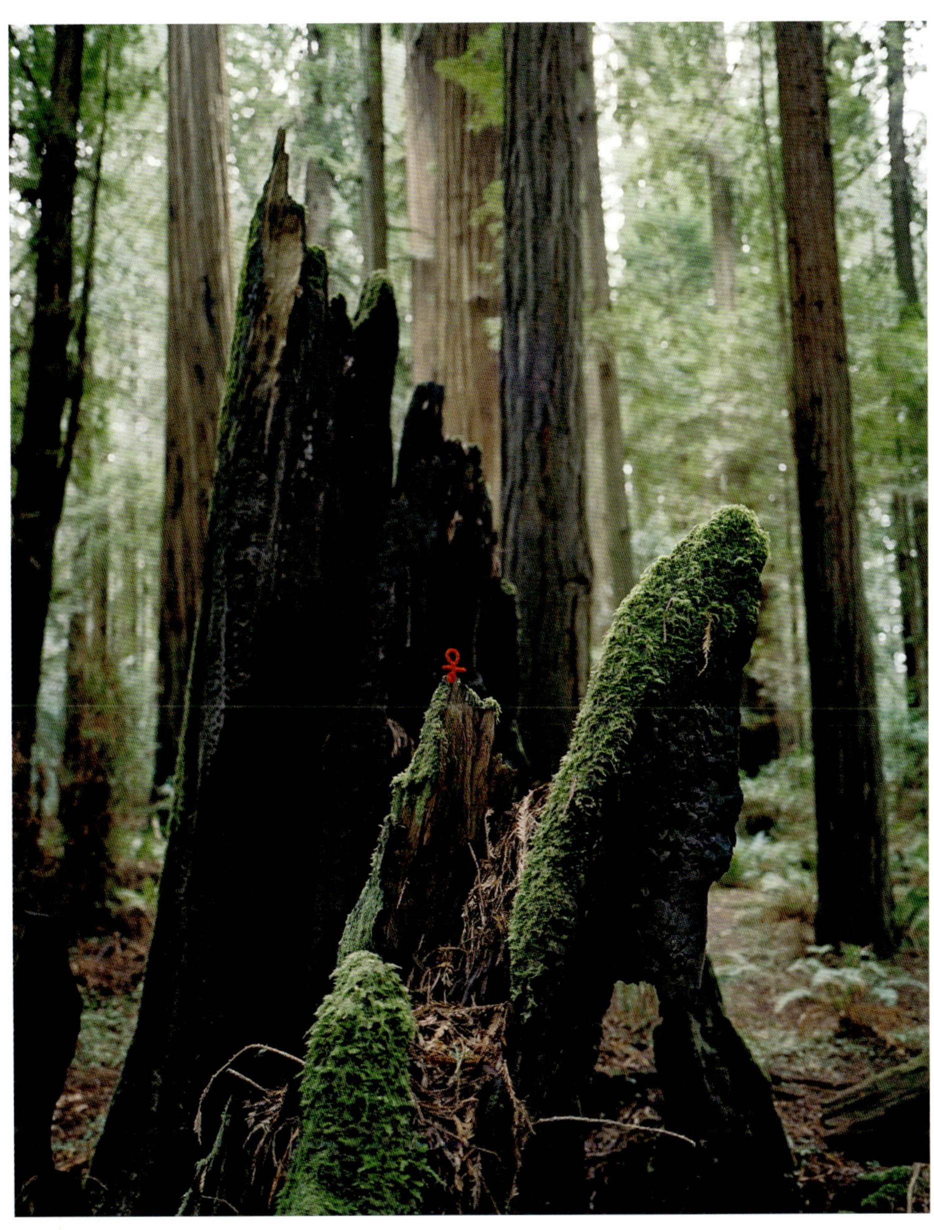

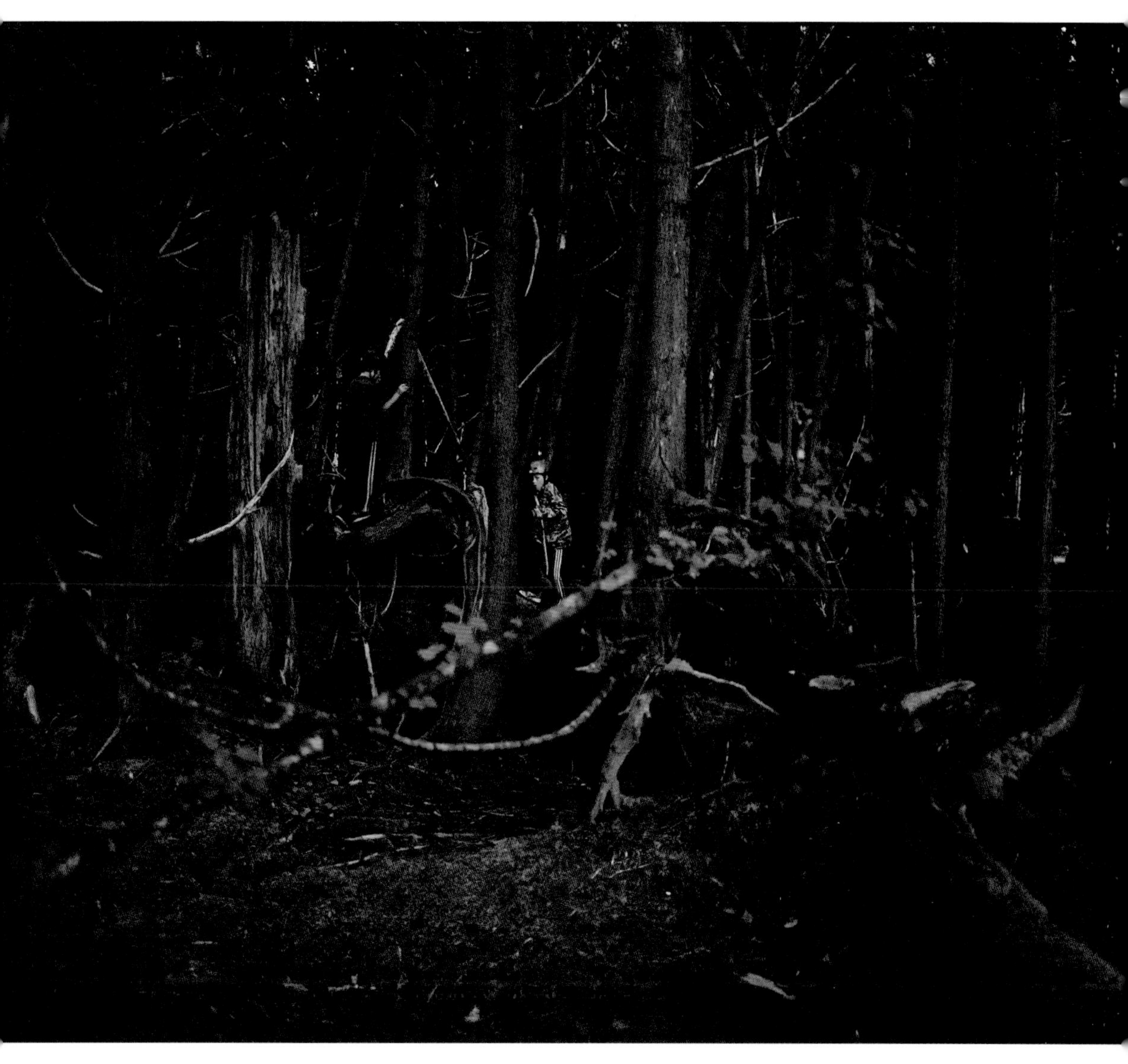

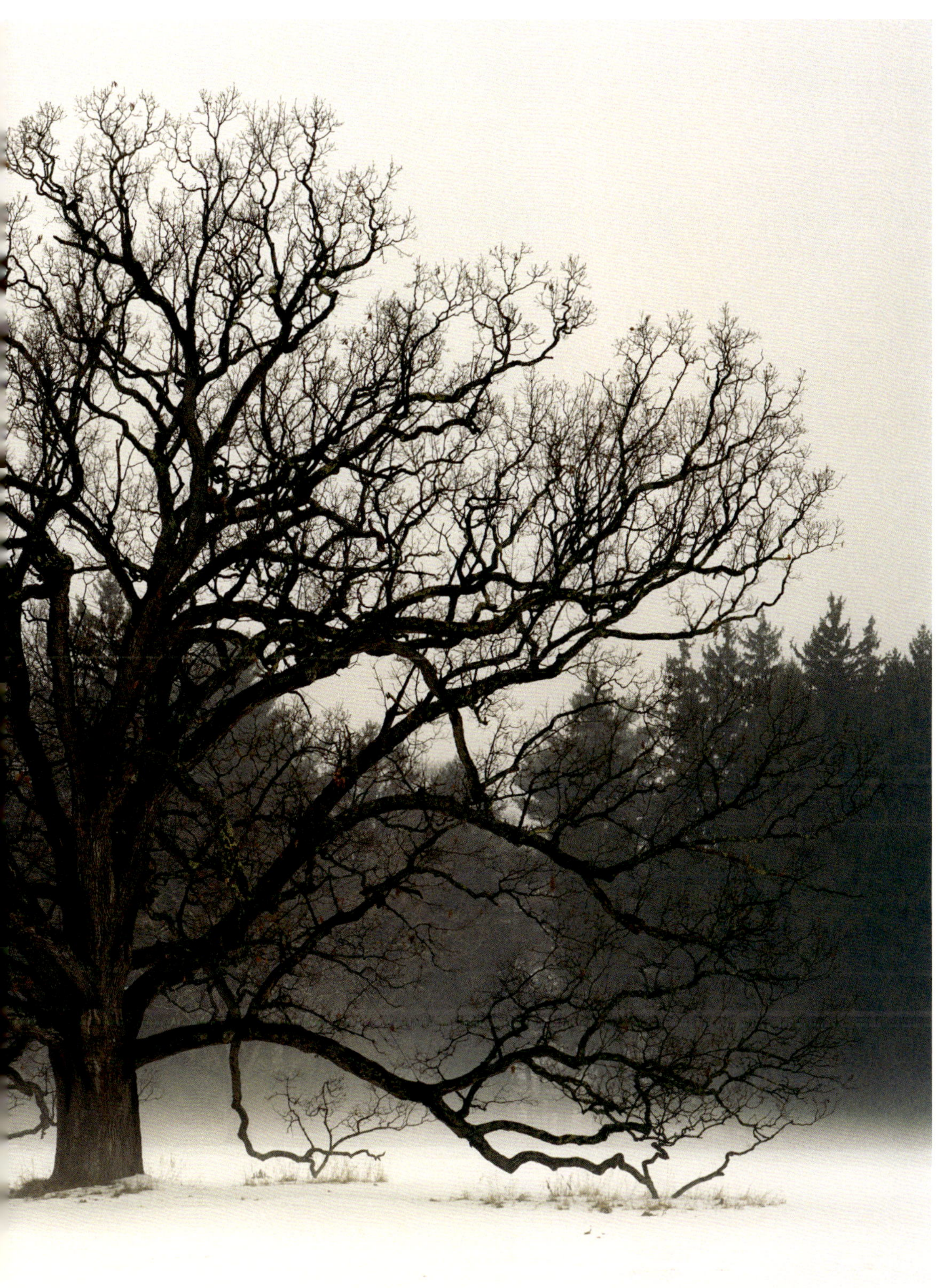

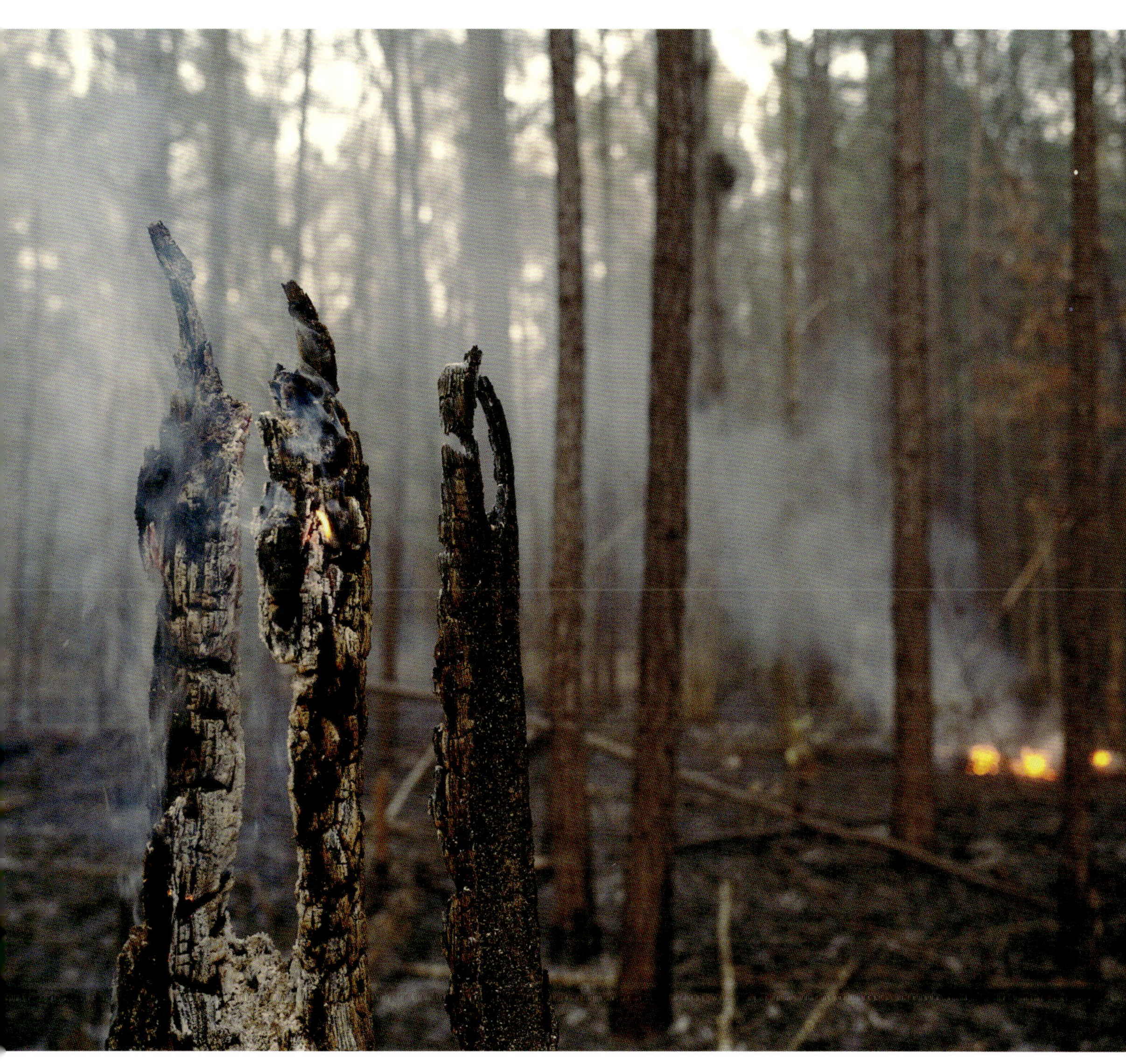

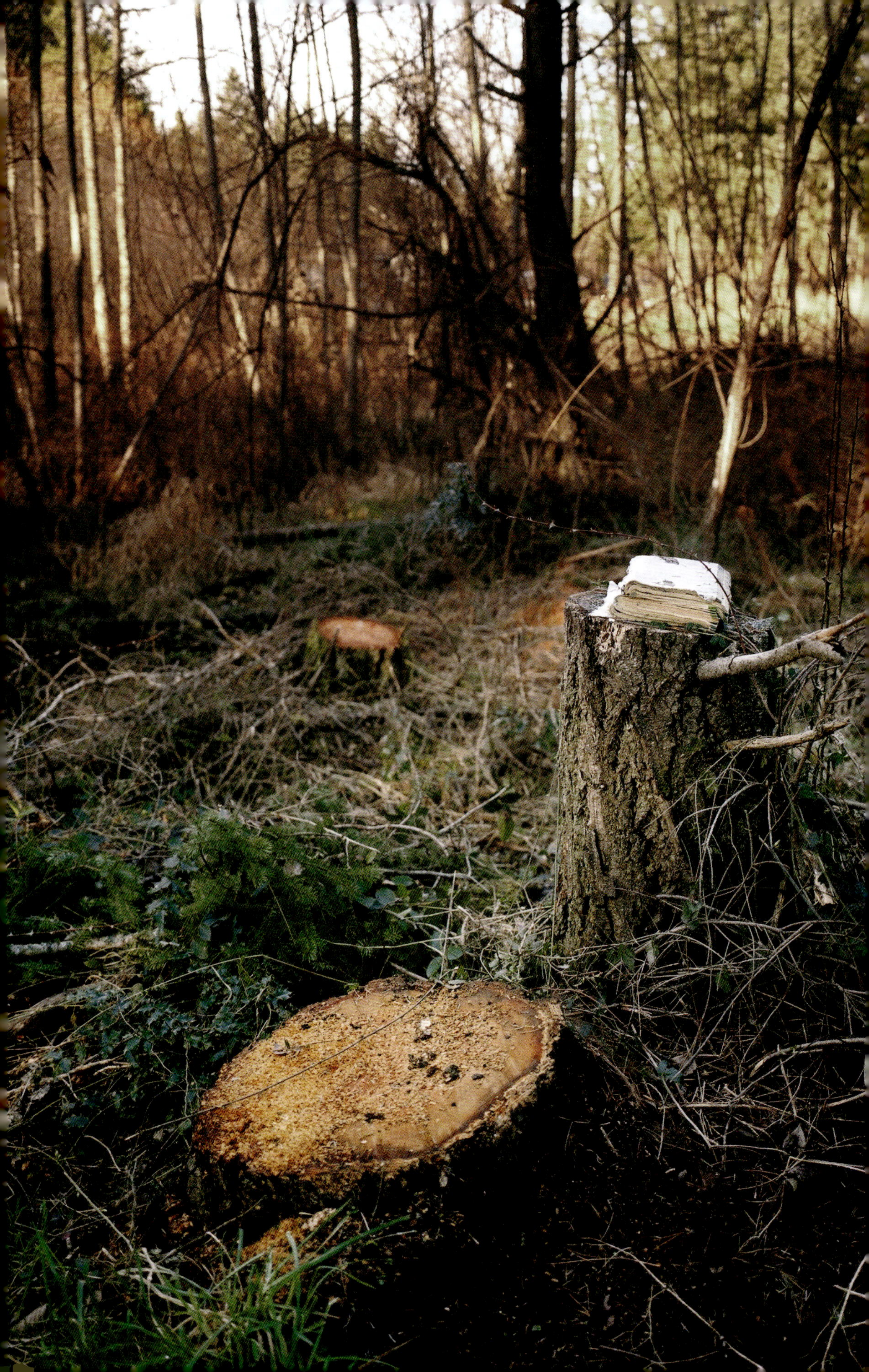

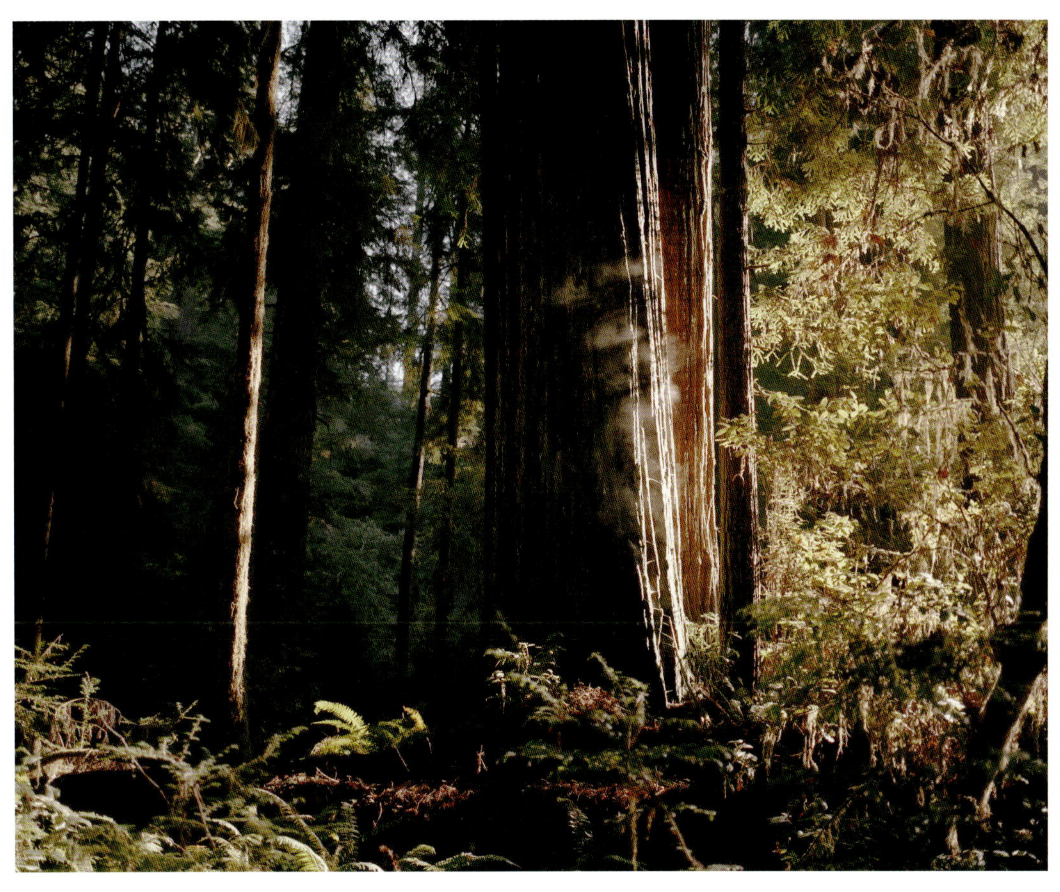

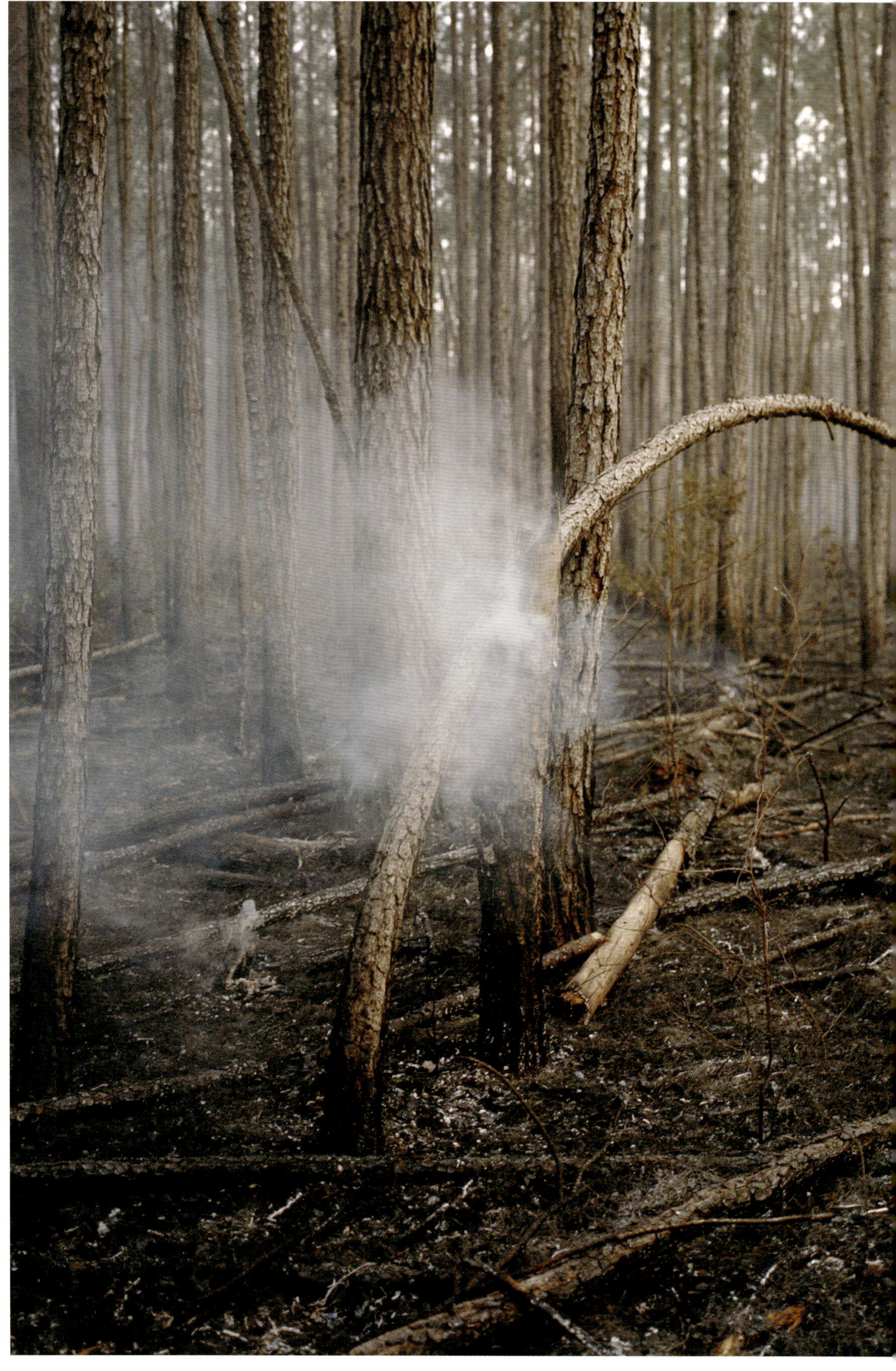

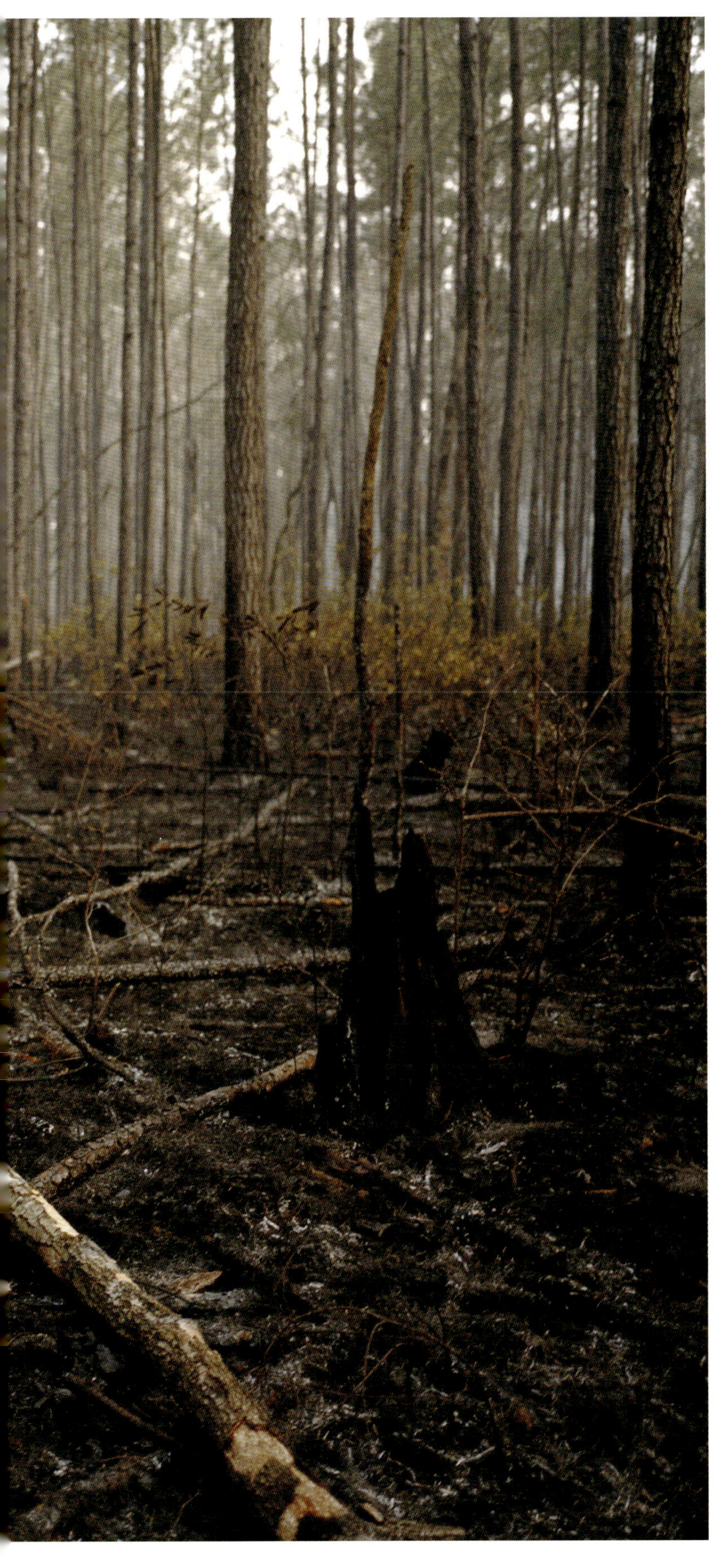

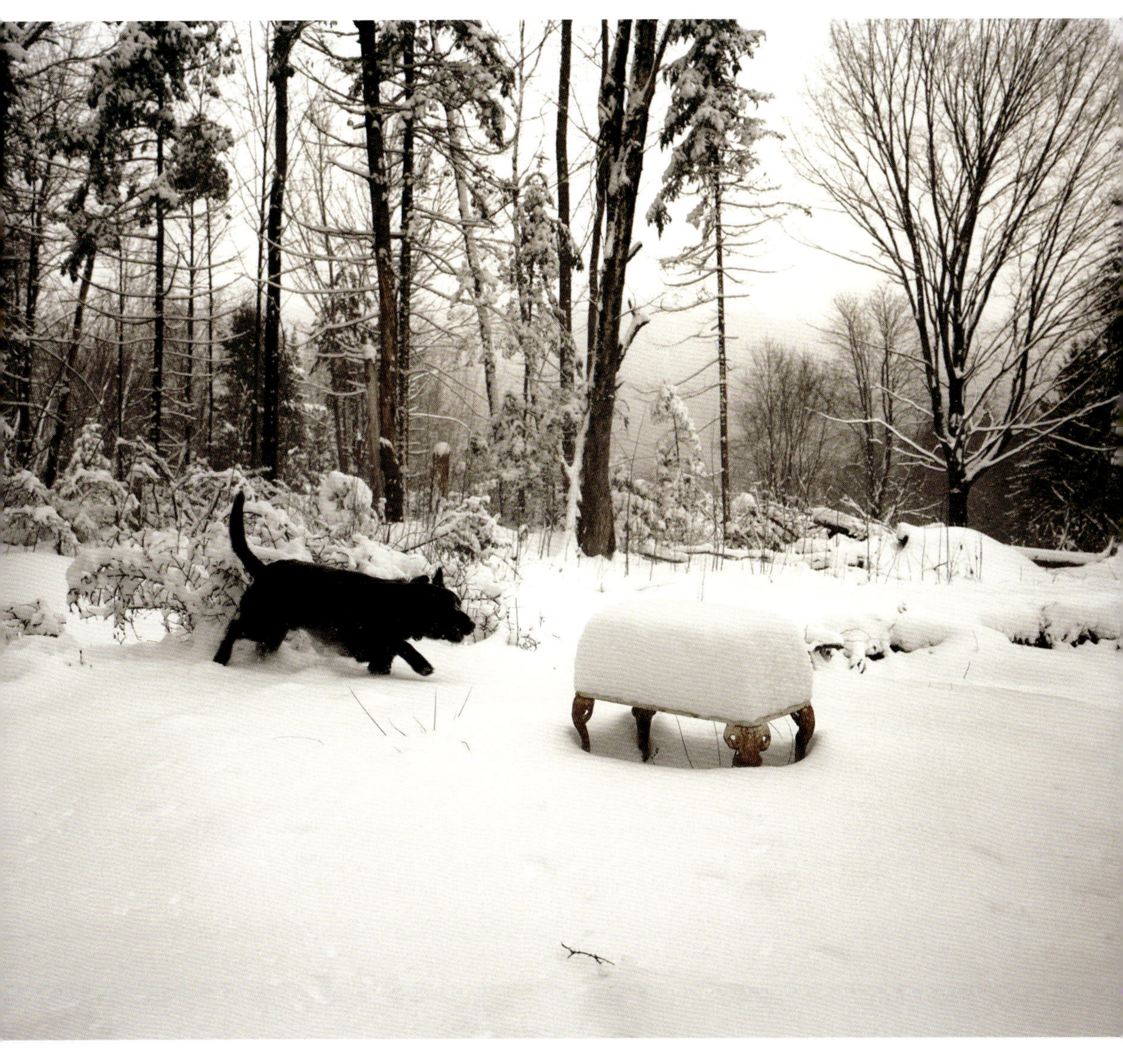

I think we are absorbed by forests and woods and thickets and copses and wilderness in general because shadows and flickering light are dangerous and alluring and mysterious. There are stories in the shadows, in the forest, flitting through the trees. How many legends and fables and myths are set in the forest? The forest is where possible lives. The forest is beyond the reach of sense and

reason. The forest is not a place for logic and culture and civilized opinion. The forest is ancient and itself. The forest is hidden life and deeper secrets. Anything might live there and probably does and the only way to find out is to slip in beneath the eaves and vanish into it in exactly the same way you vanish into a story.

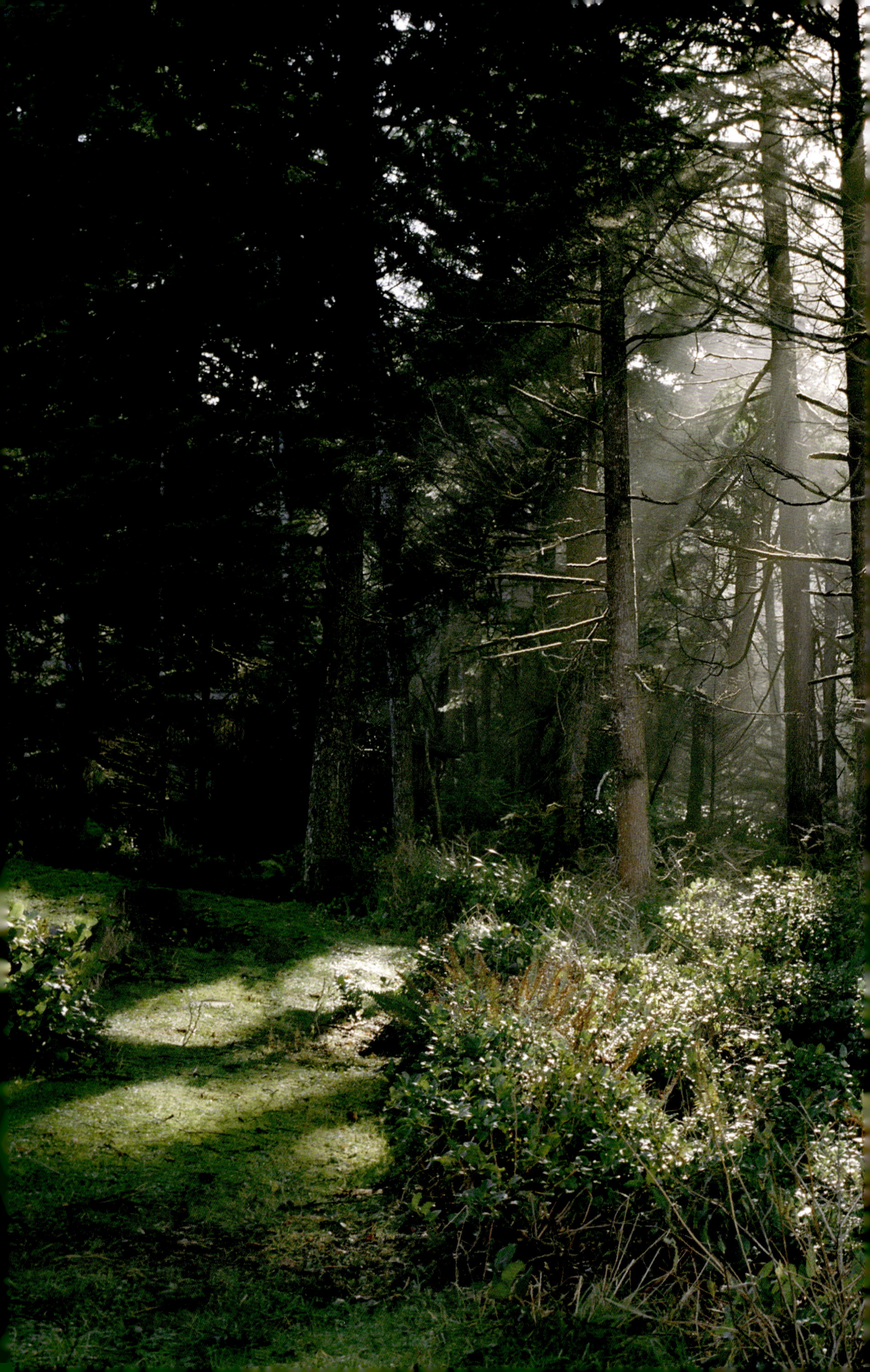

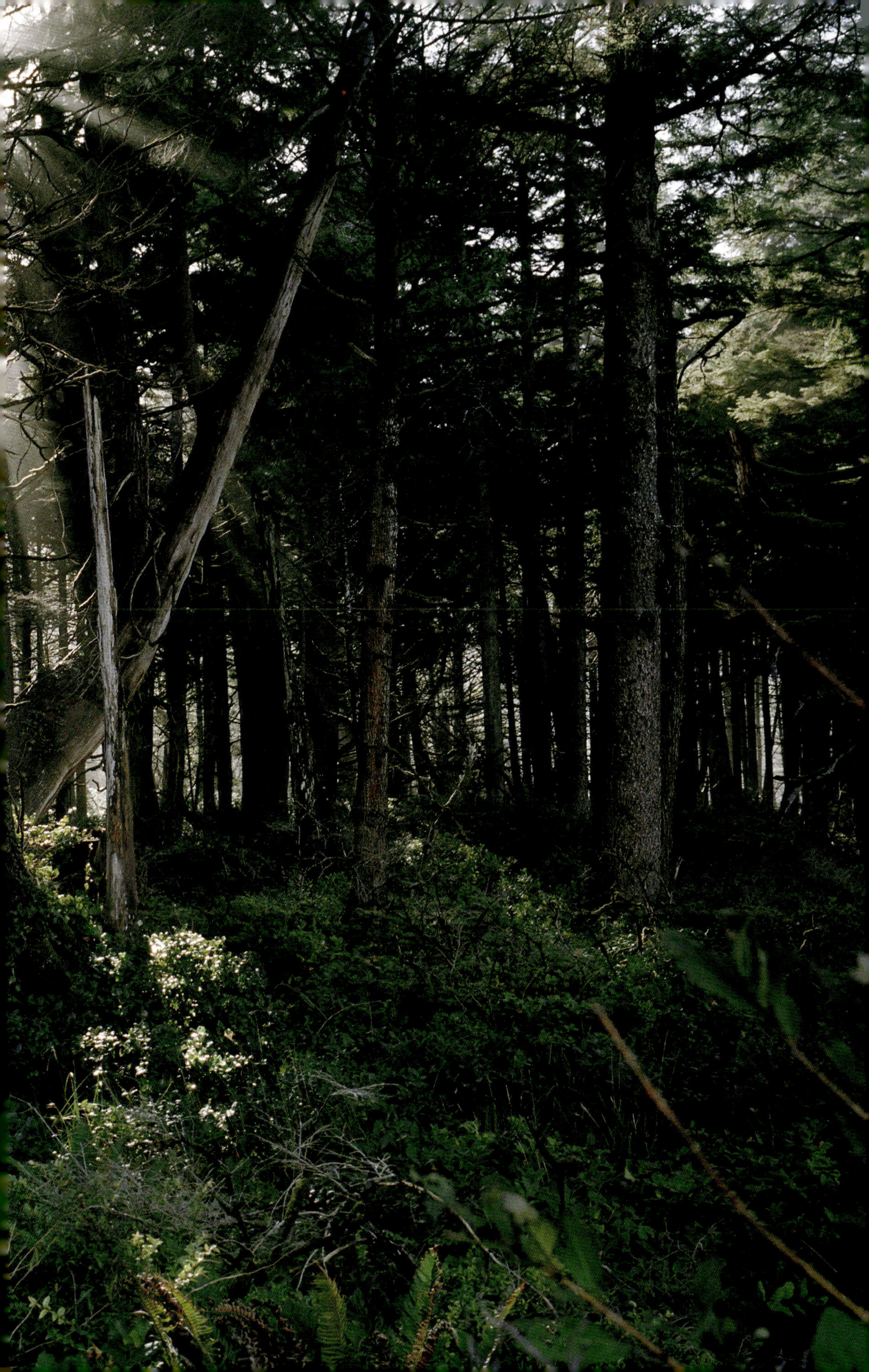

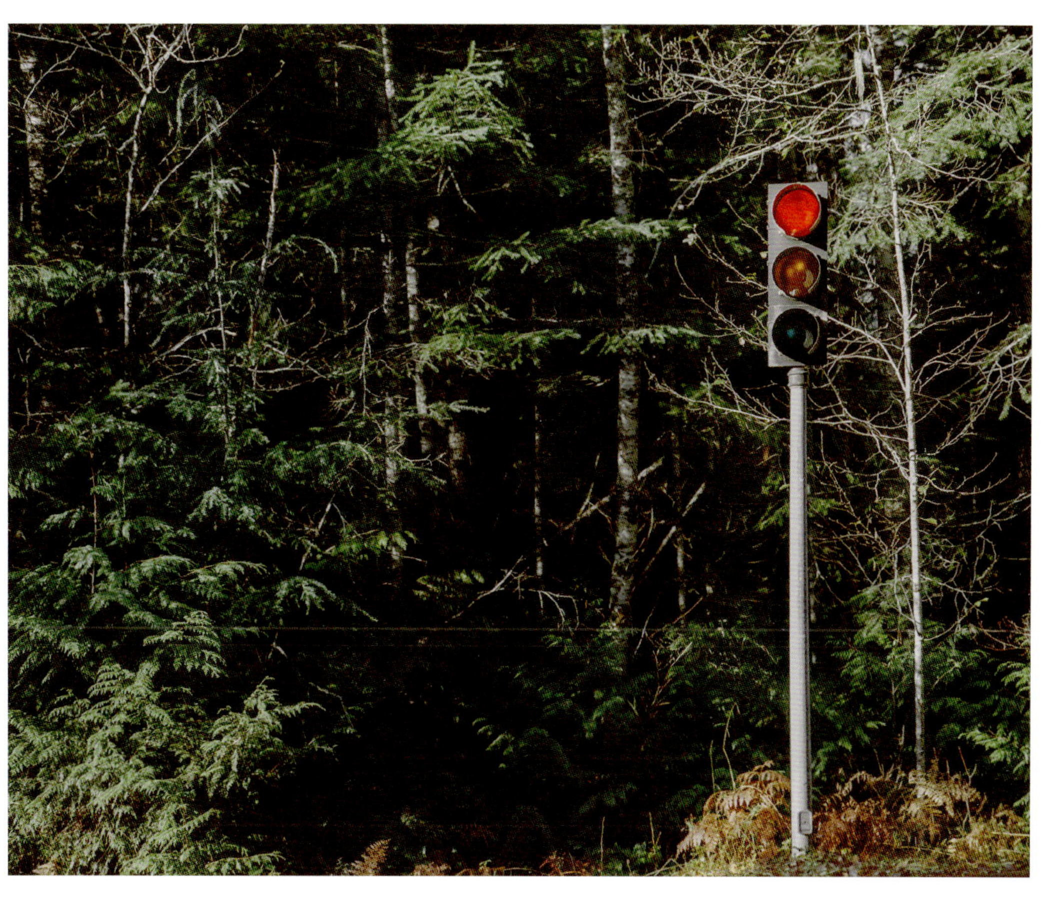

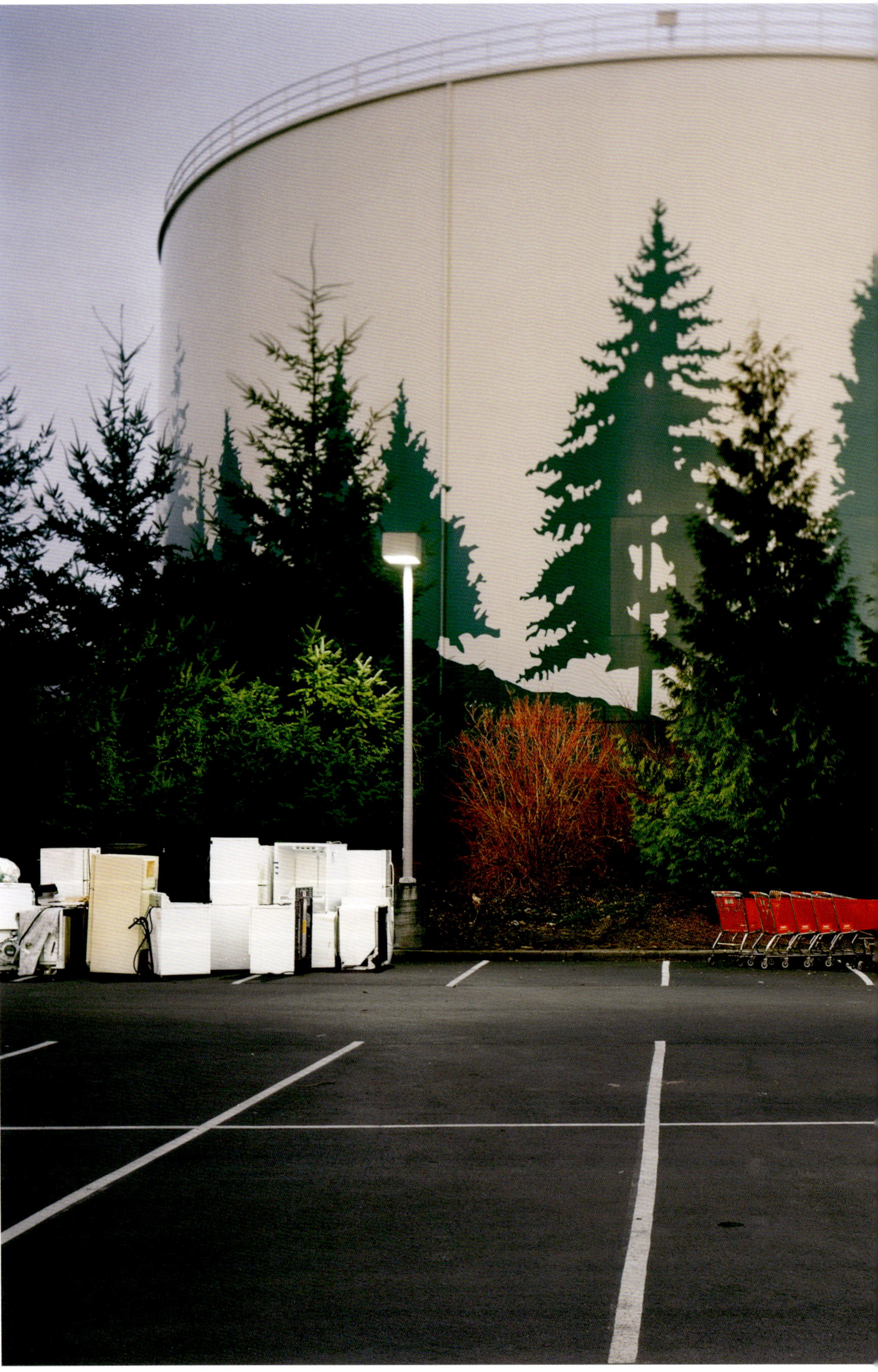

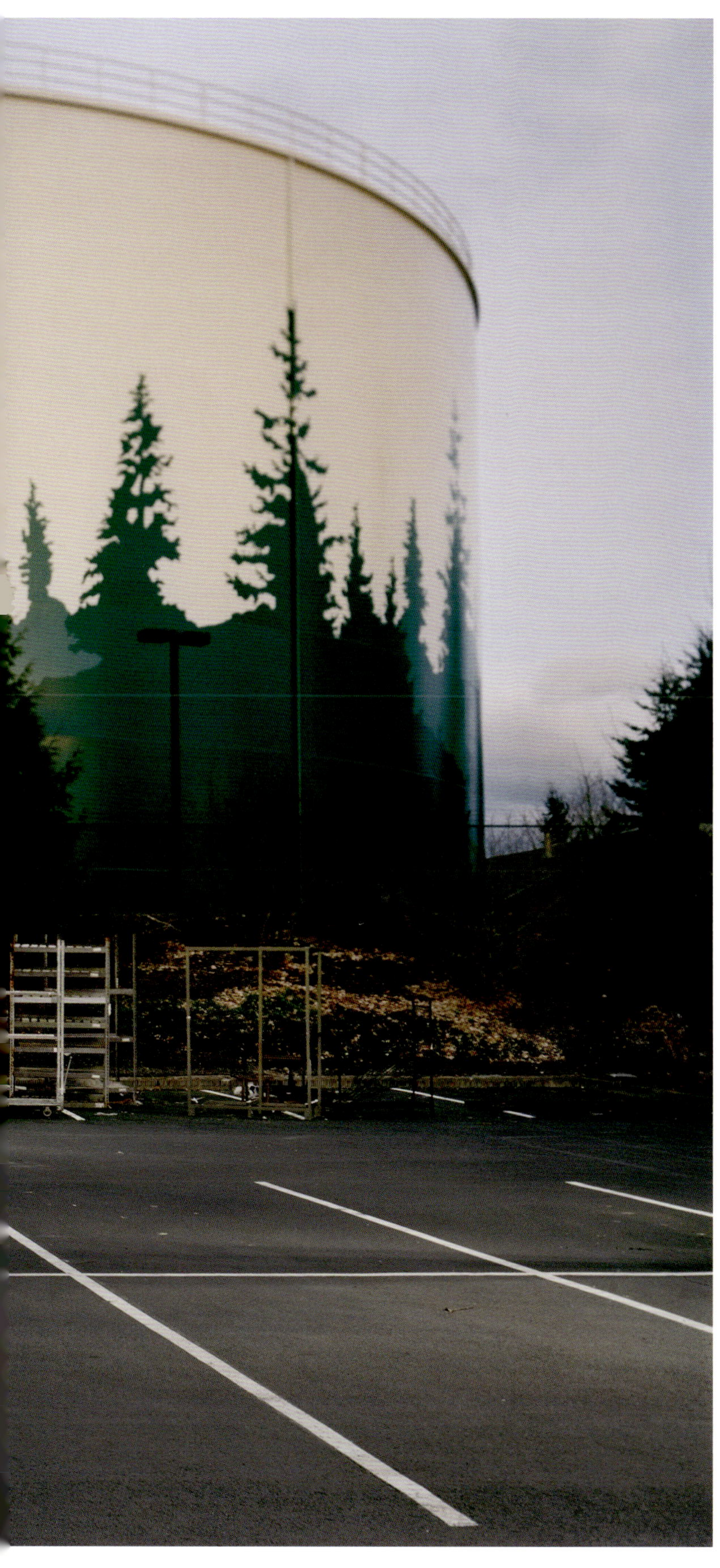

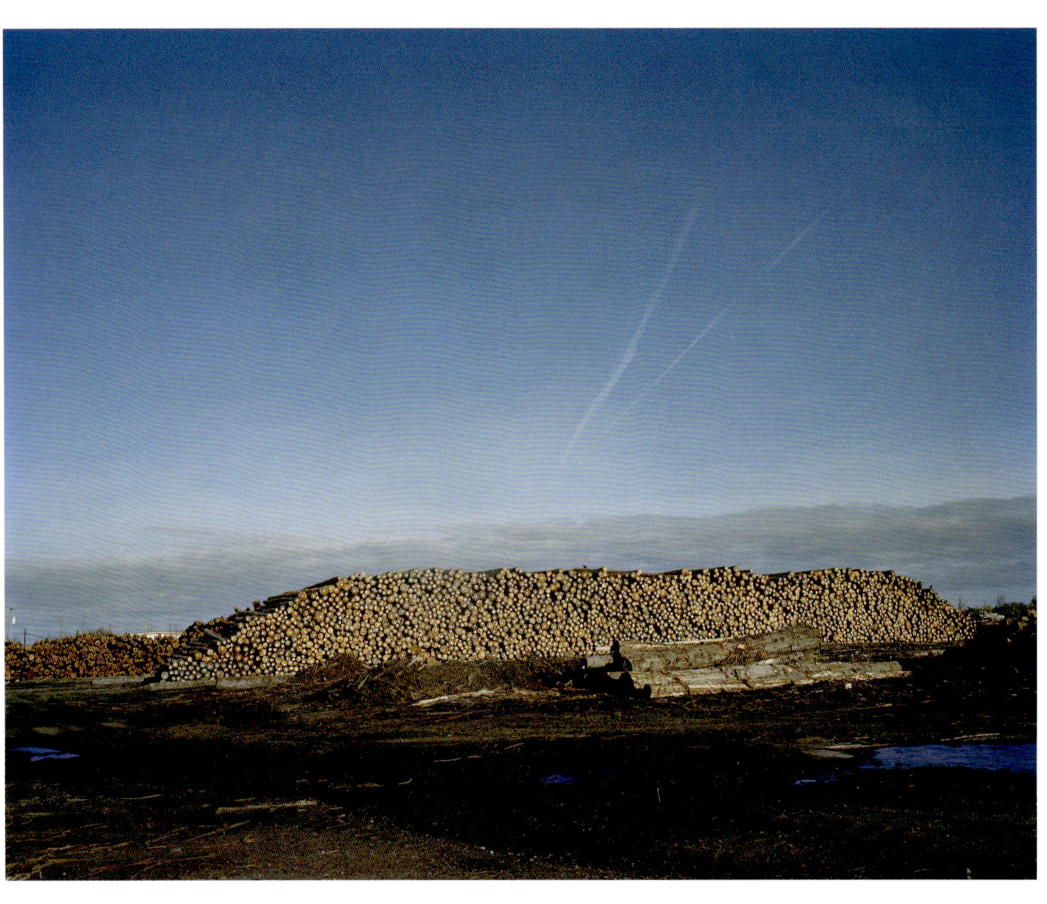

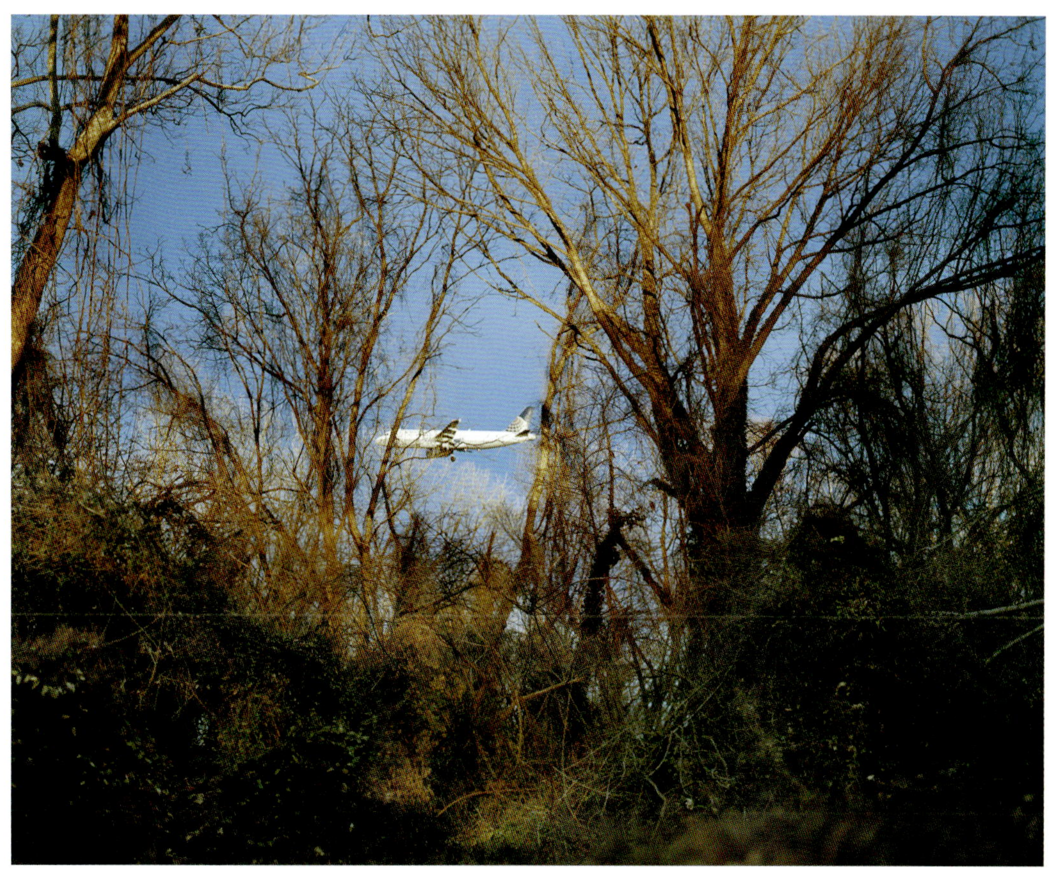

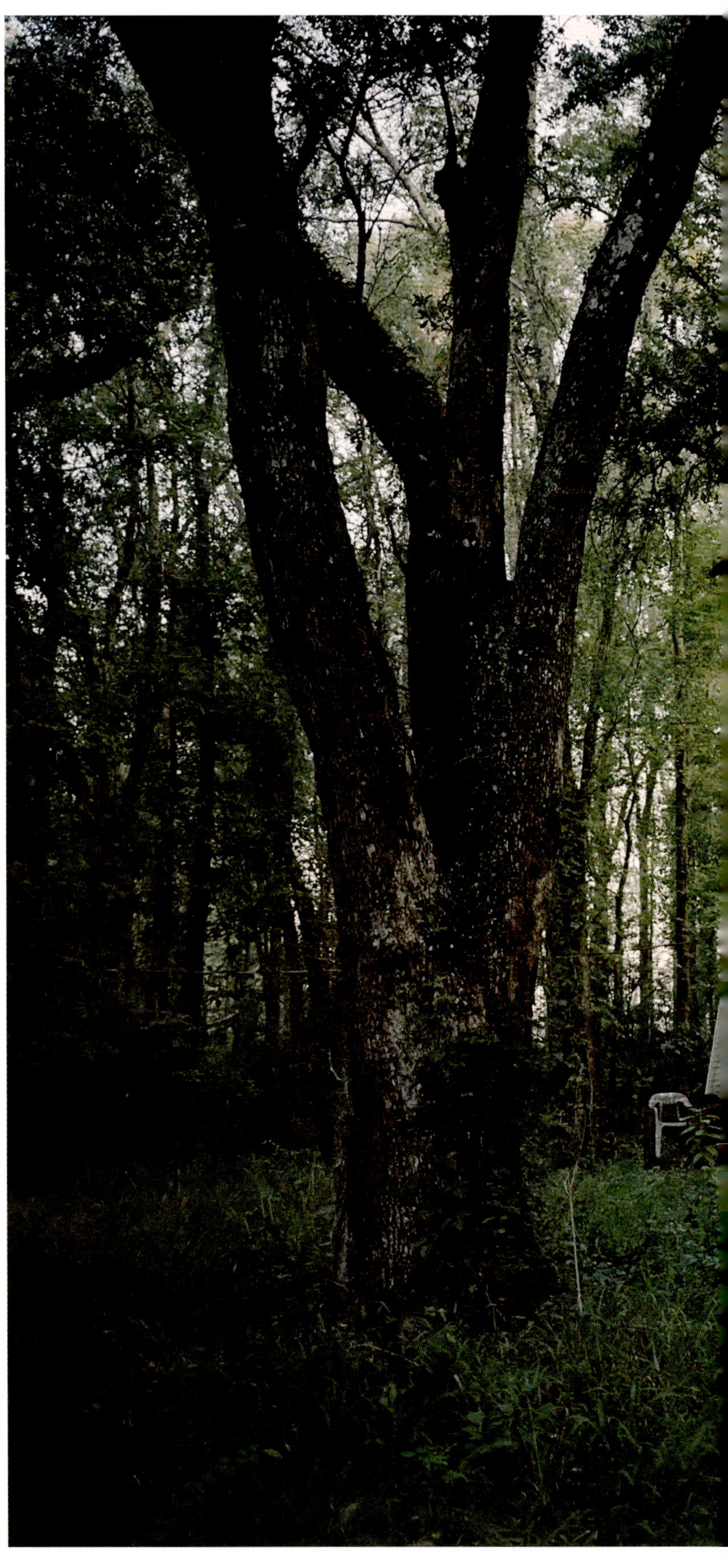

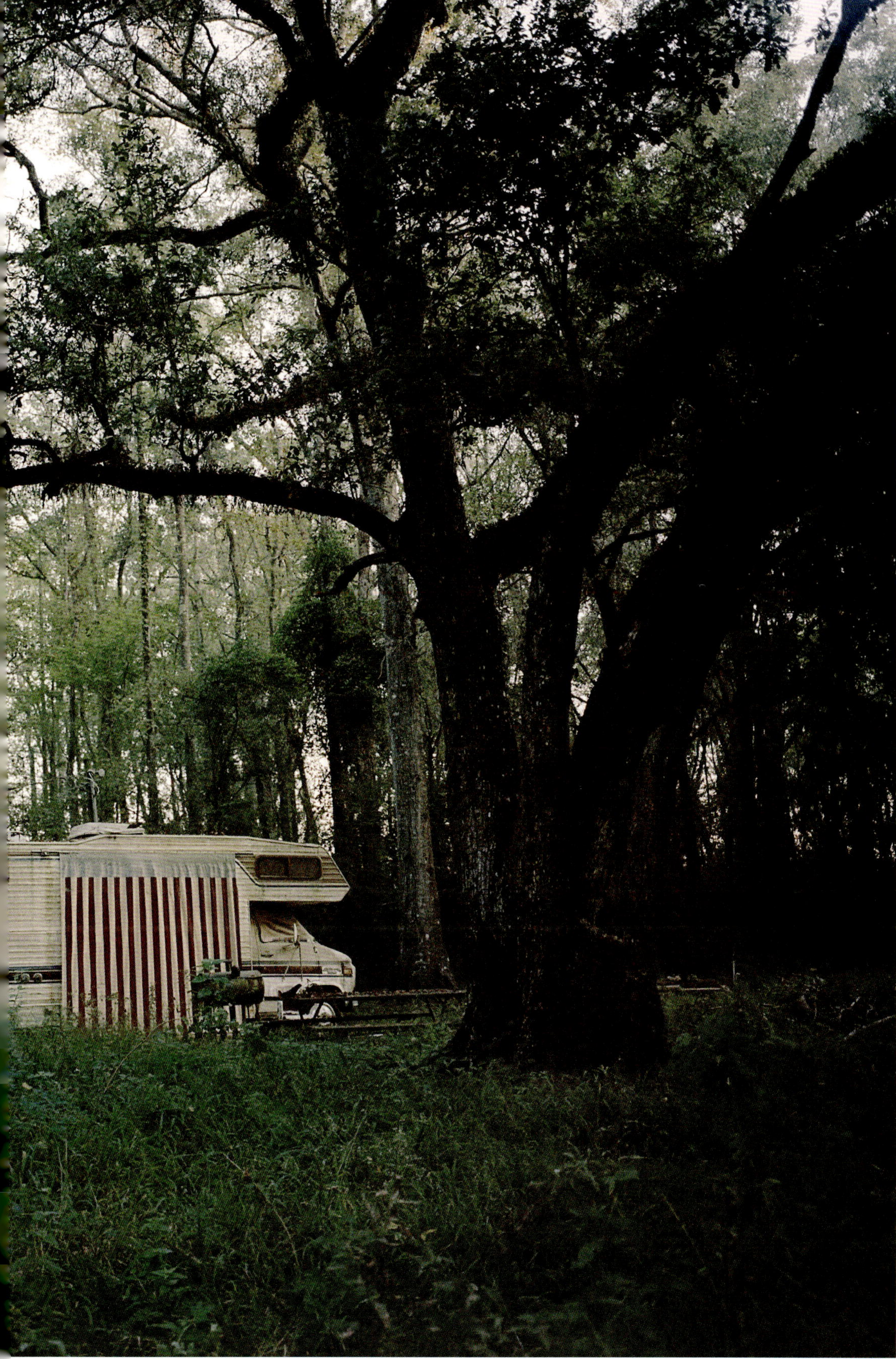

As a species, said the late great Peter Matthiessen once, we are just down from the trees. We used to live in the trees. We forget that. We came down from the trees and out onto the savannah and we are still afraid of death. We are still filled with fear. That's why we are so violent. We lash out. What if our moral evolution ever caught up to our astounding physical evolution? What then?

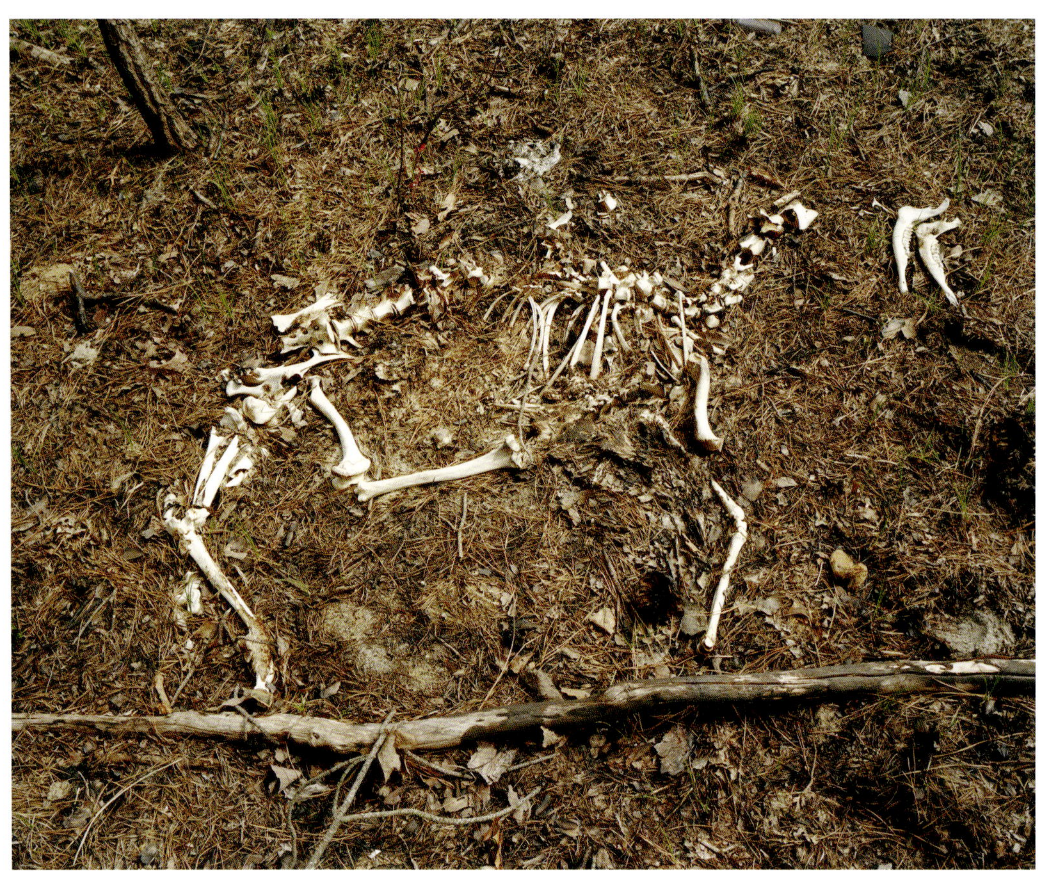

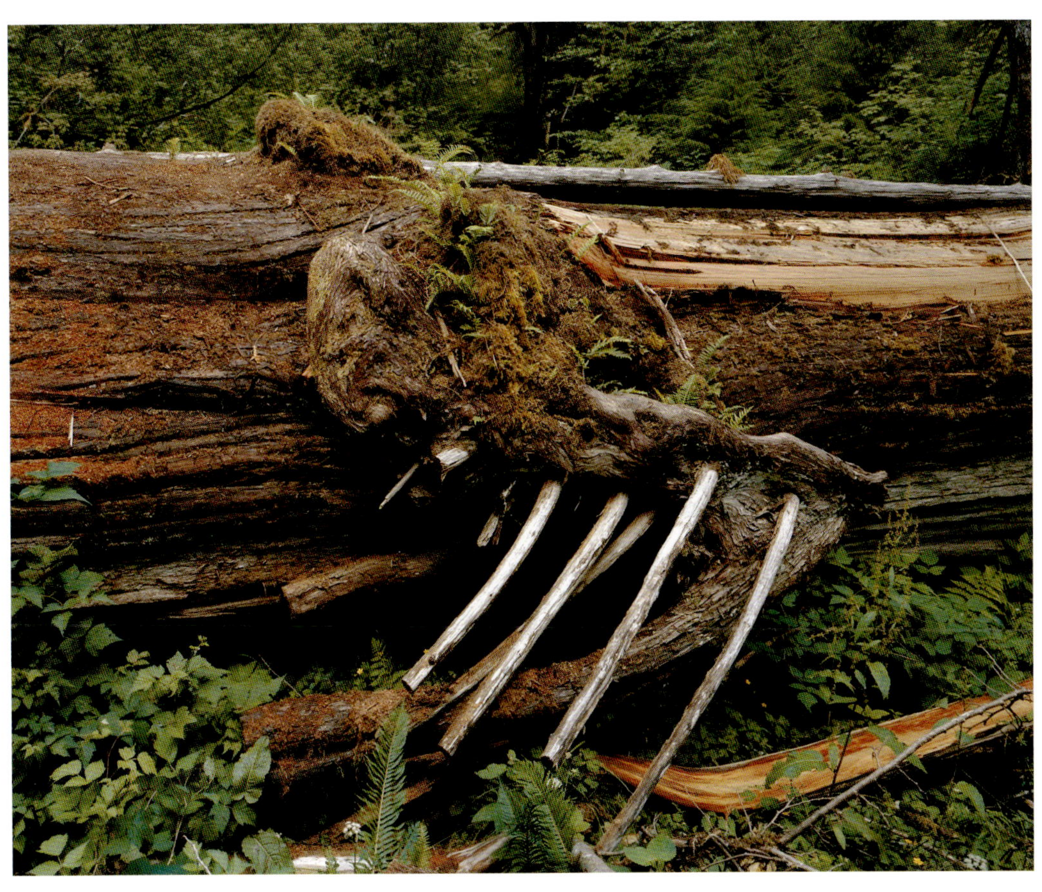

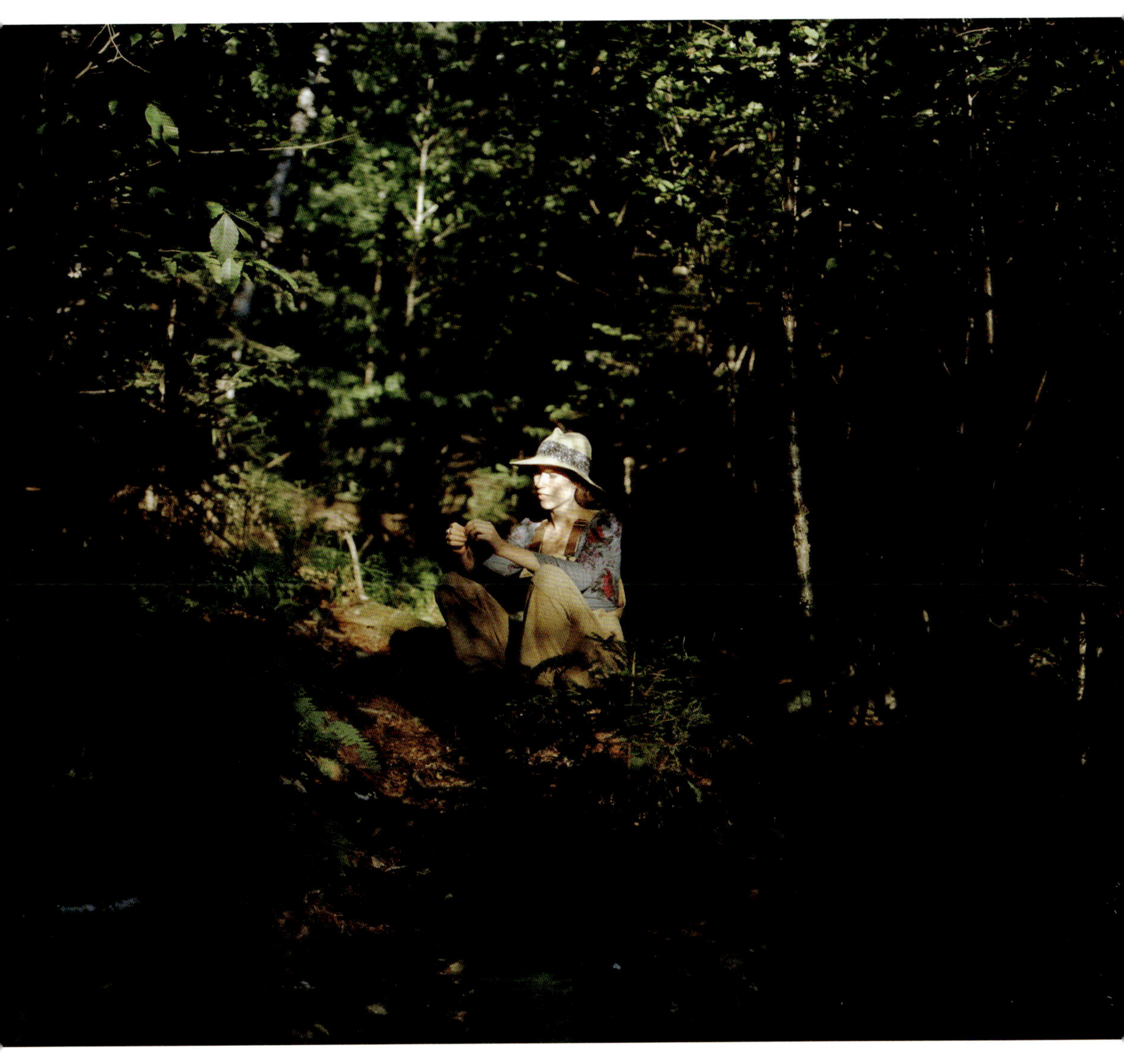

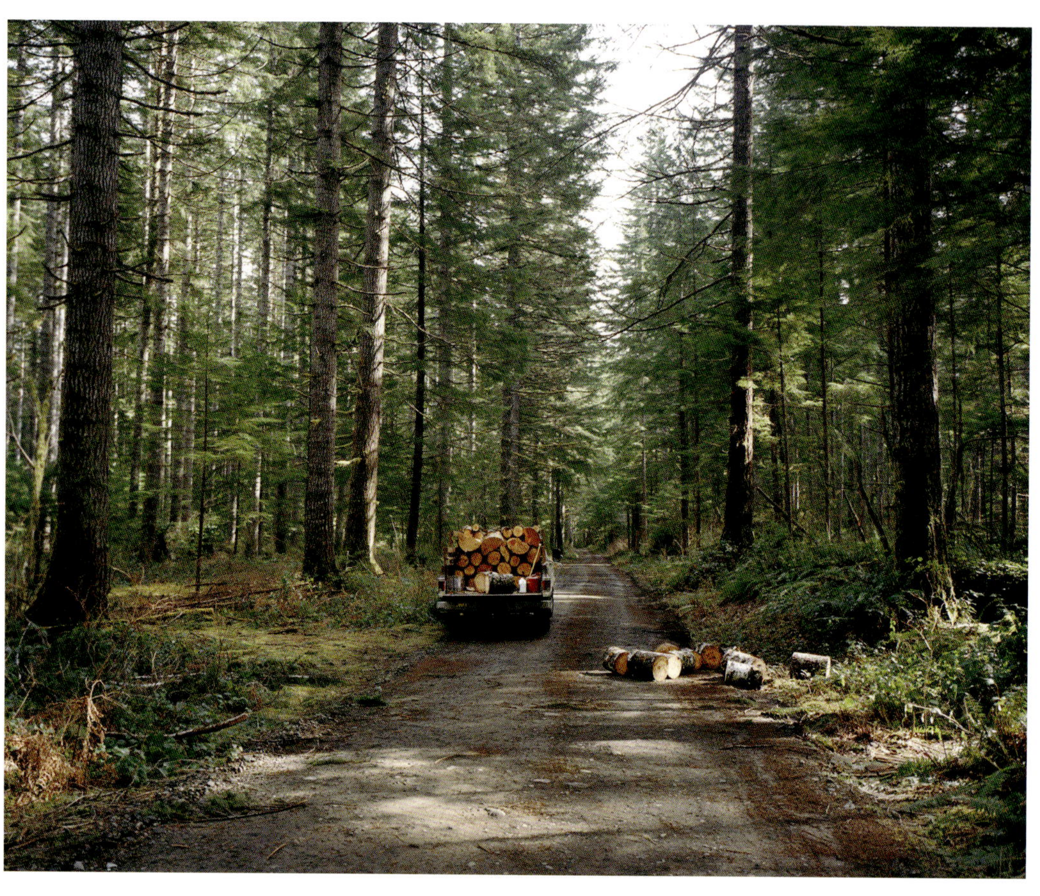

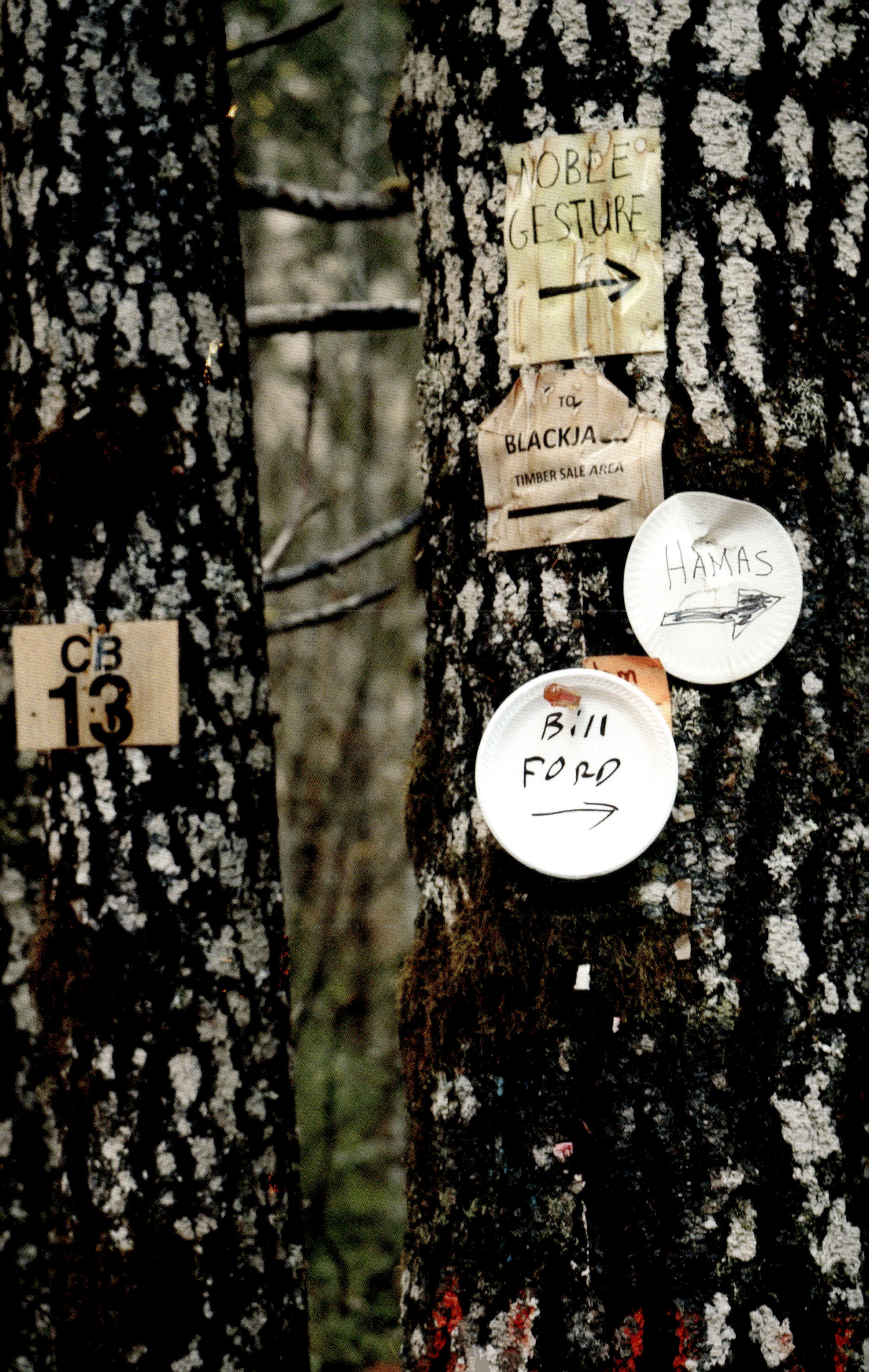
NOBLE GESTURE
TO
BLACKJA
TIMBER SALE AREA
HAMAS
Bill FORD
CB 13

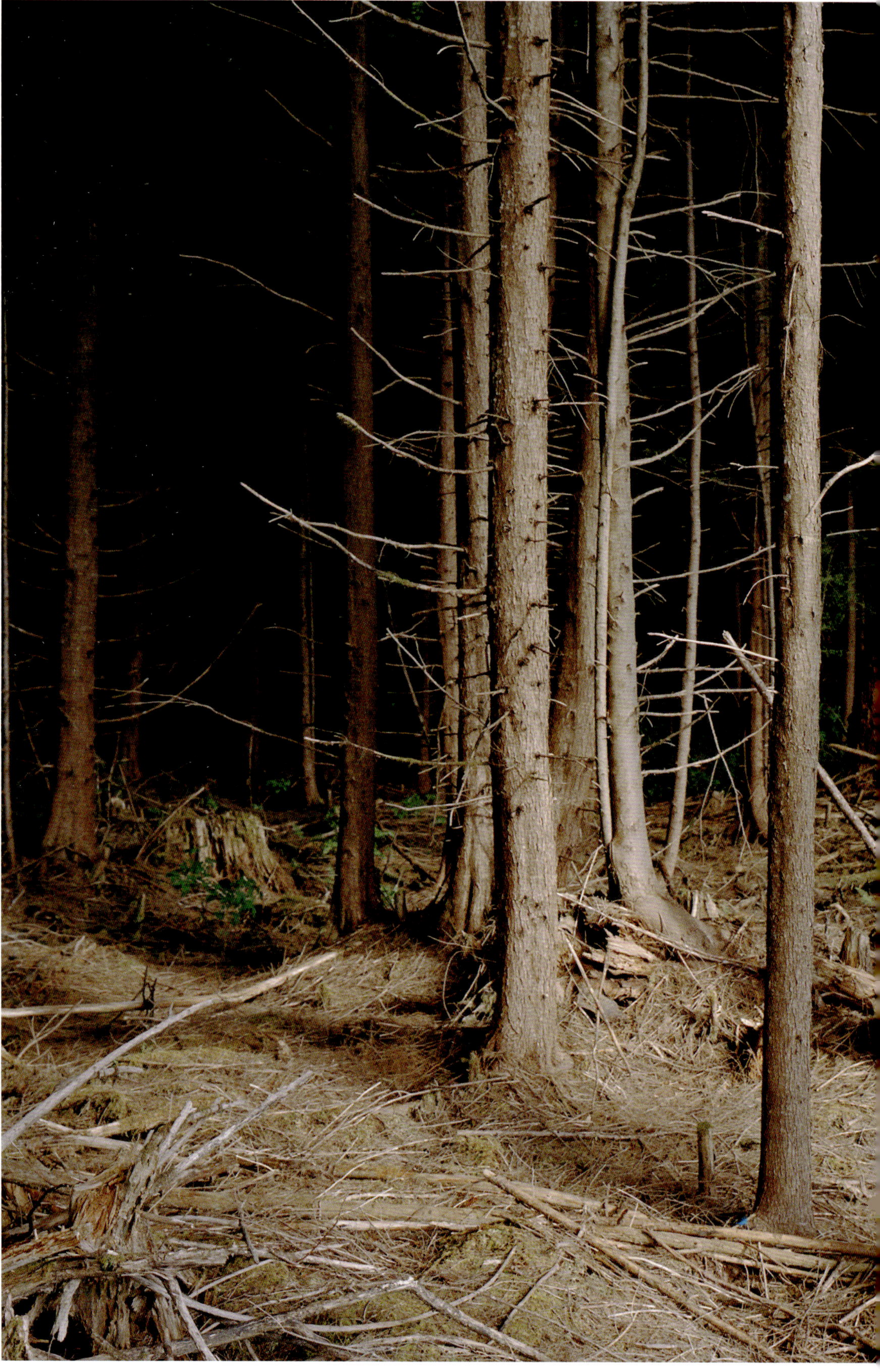

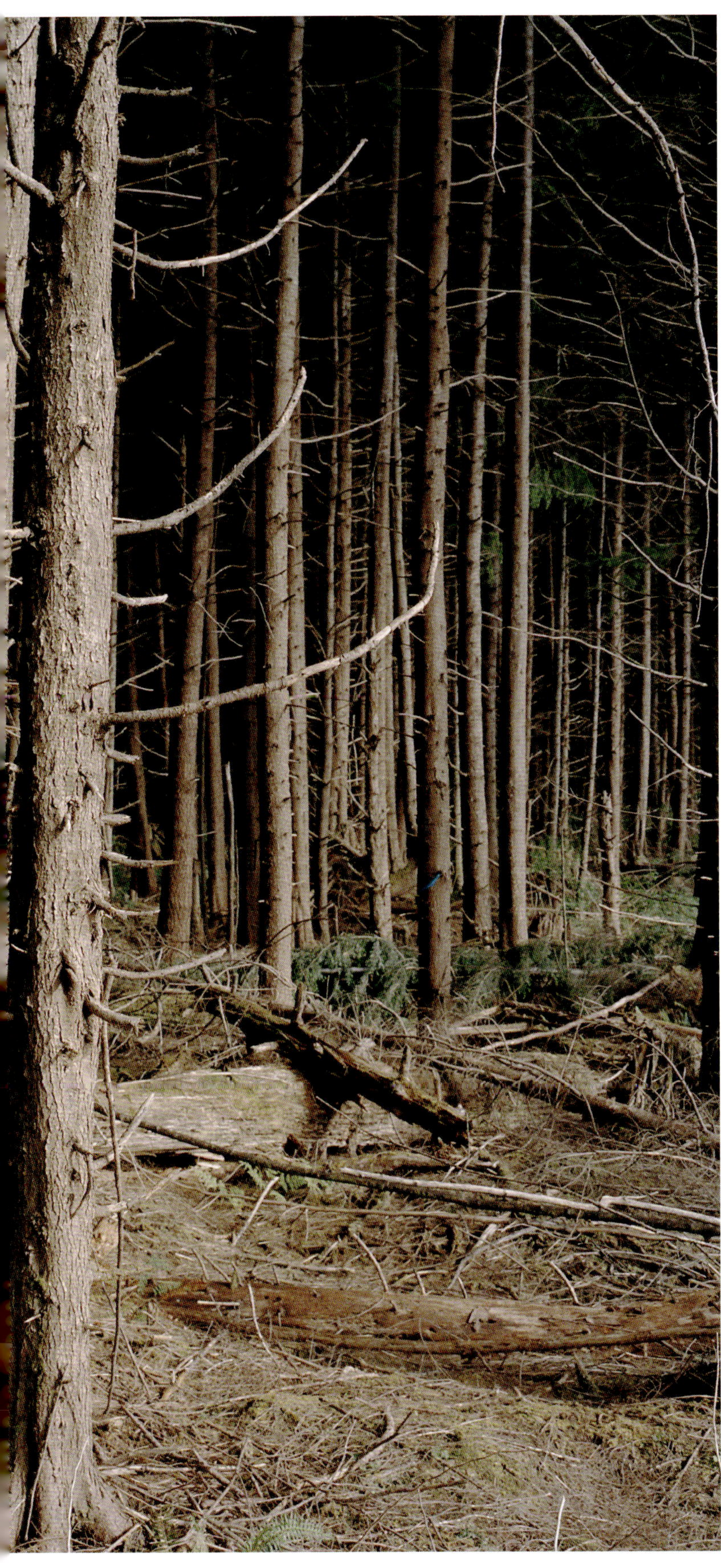

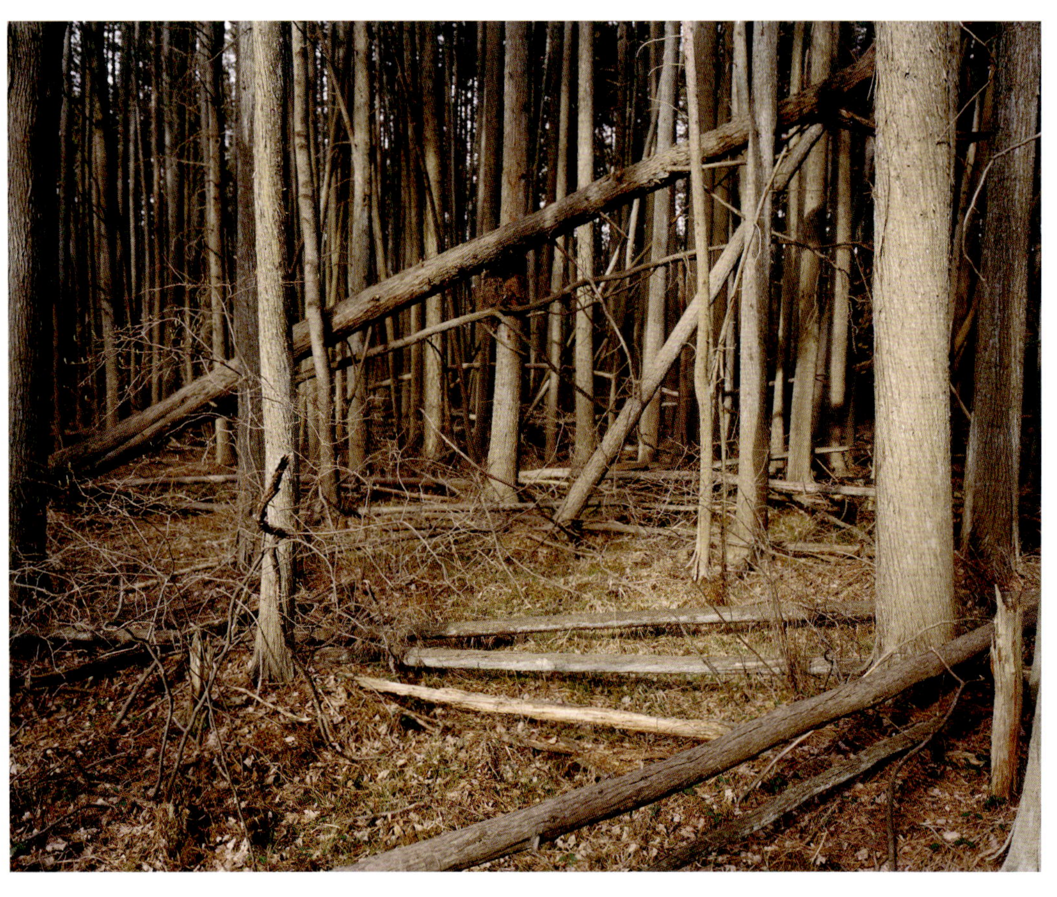

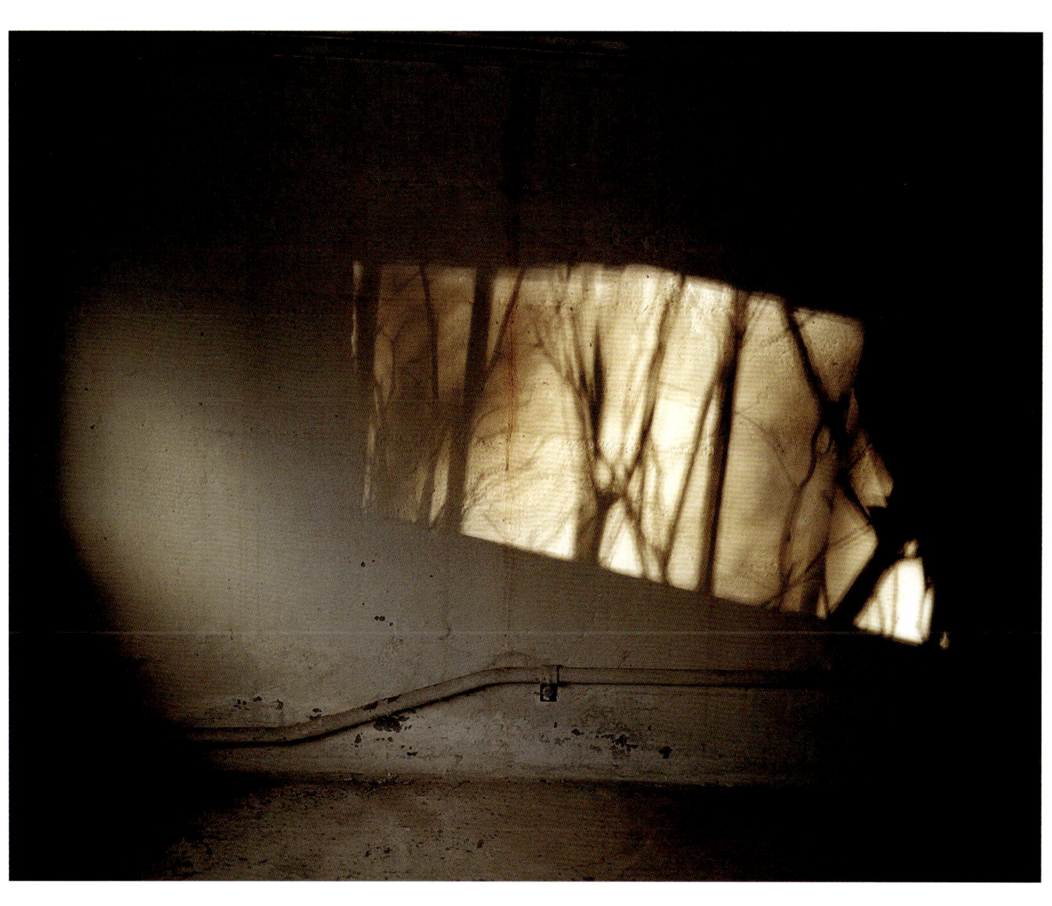

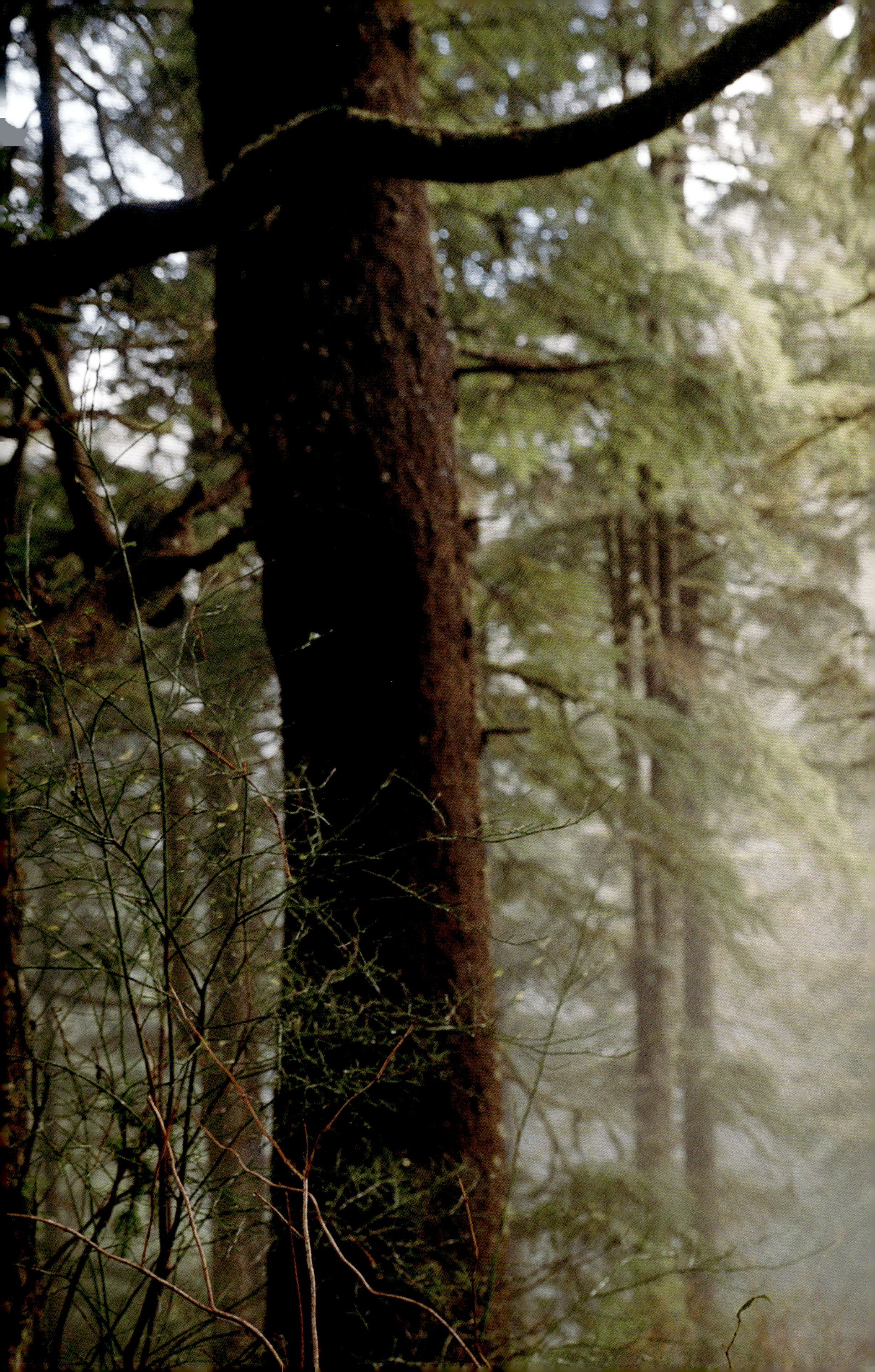

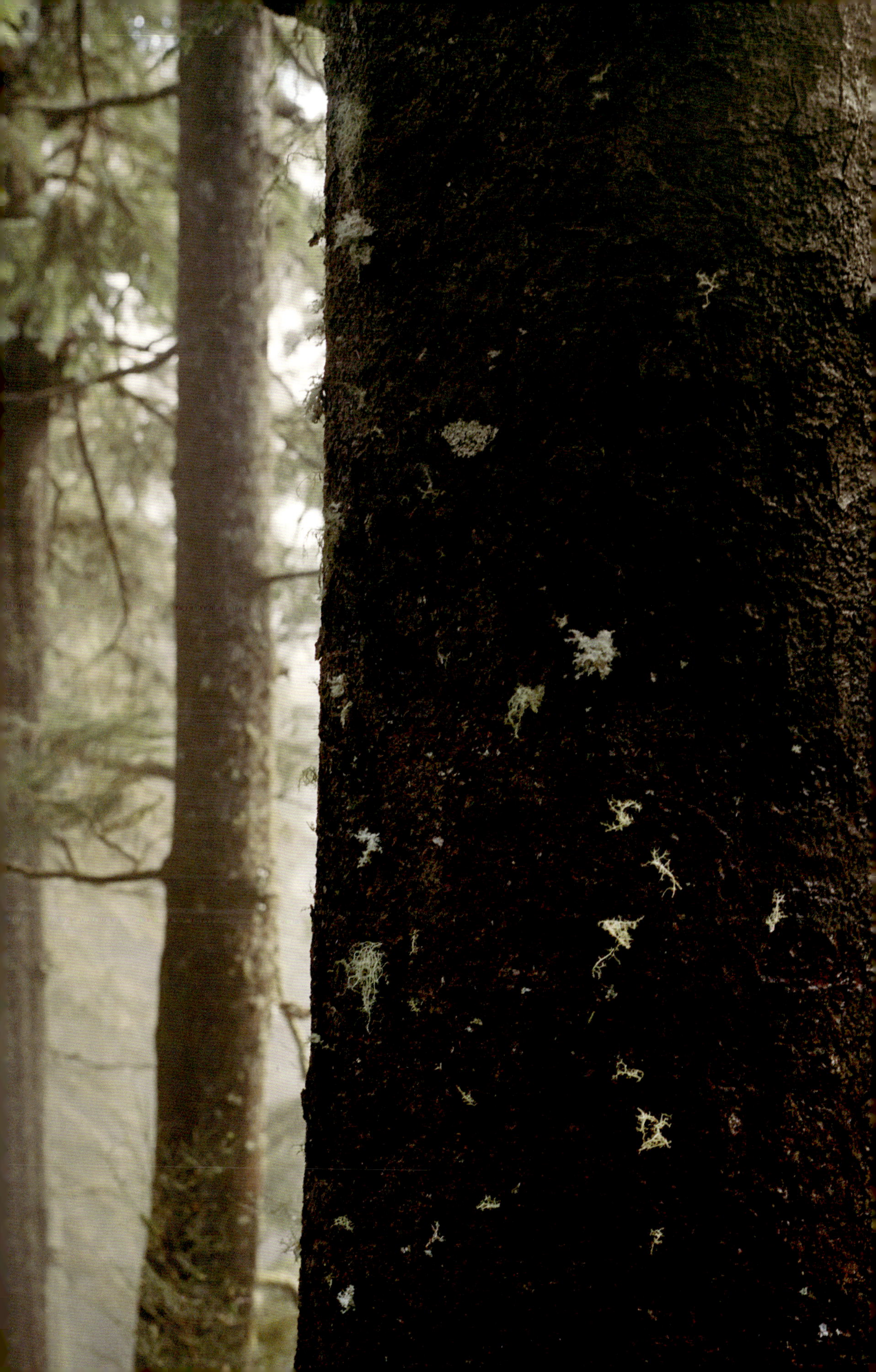

The biggest tree I ever saw personally myself, on foot, not from the road with other sightseers and erudite rangers and park authorities, was a spruce on the Oregon coast. You wouldn't believe how fat and tall this tree was. It was so much bigger than your house that your house would quail a little if they were on the bus together. It had been measured, and its weight and age estimated, and it had been entered in registers of huge trees, and it was sort of famous, I guess, but I am here to tell you that numbers slid off this thing like small vulgar jokes. This sylvan creature – for creature it was, alive and sentient and digesting sun from above and minerals from below and water from the mist – was so big that when people saw it for the first time they went silent. How people looked when they saw it for the first time is what we mean when we say awe, it seems to me.

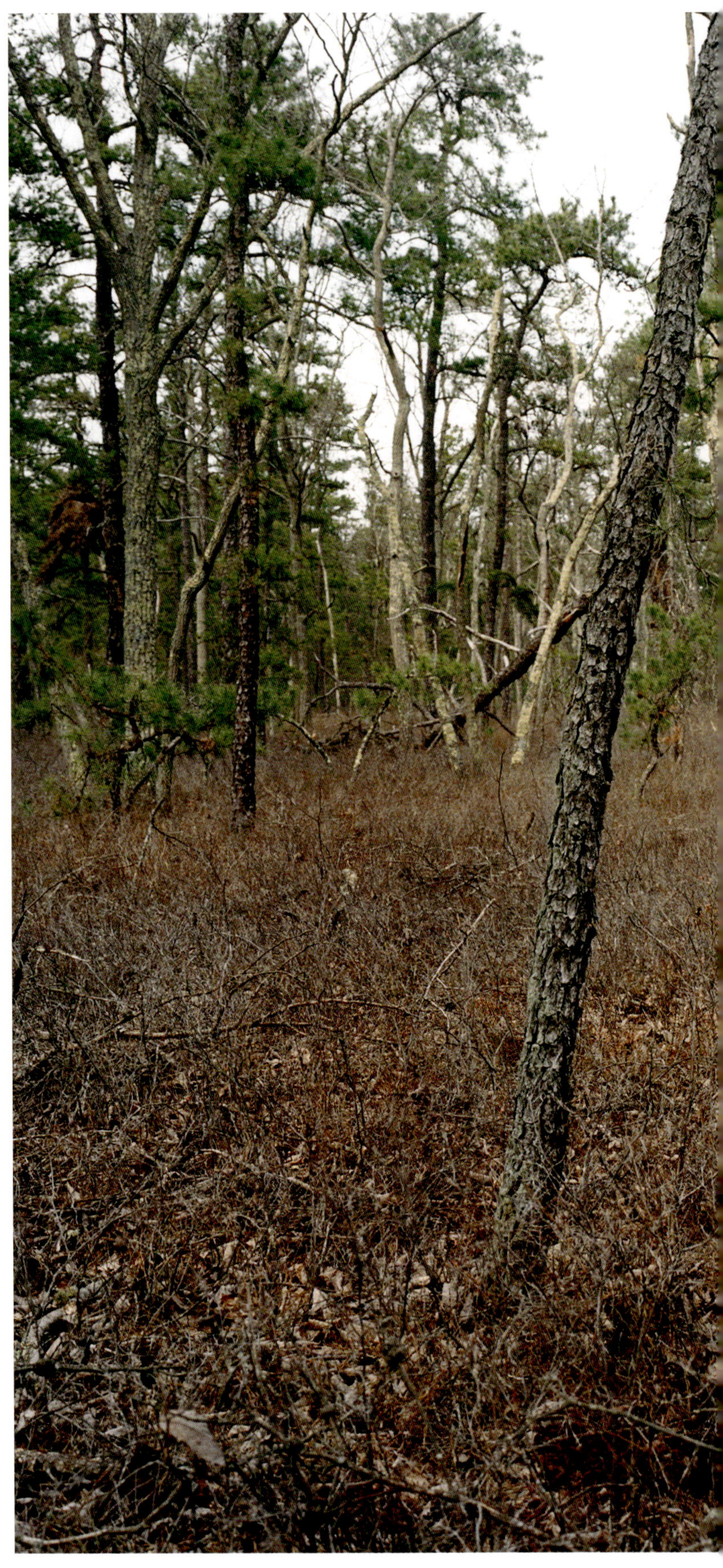

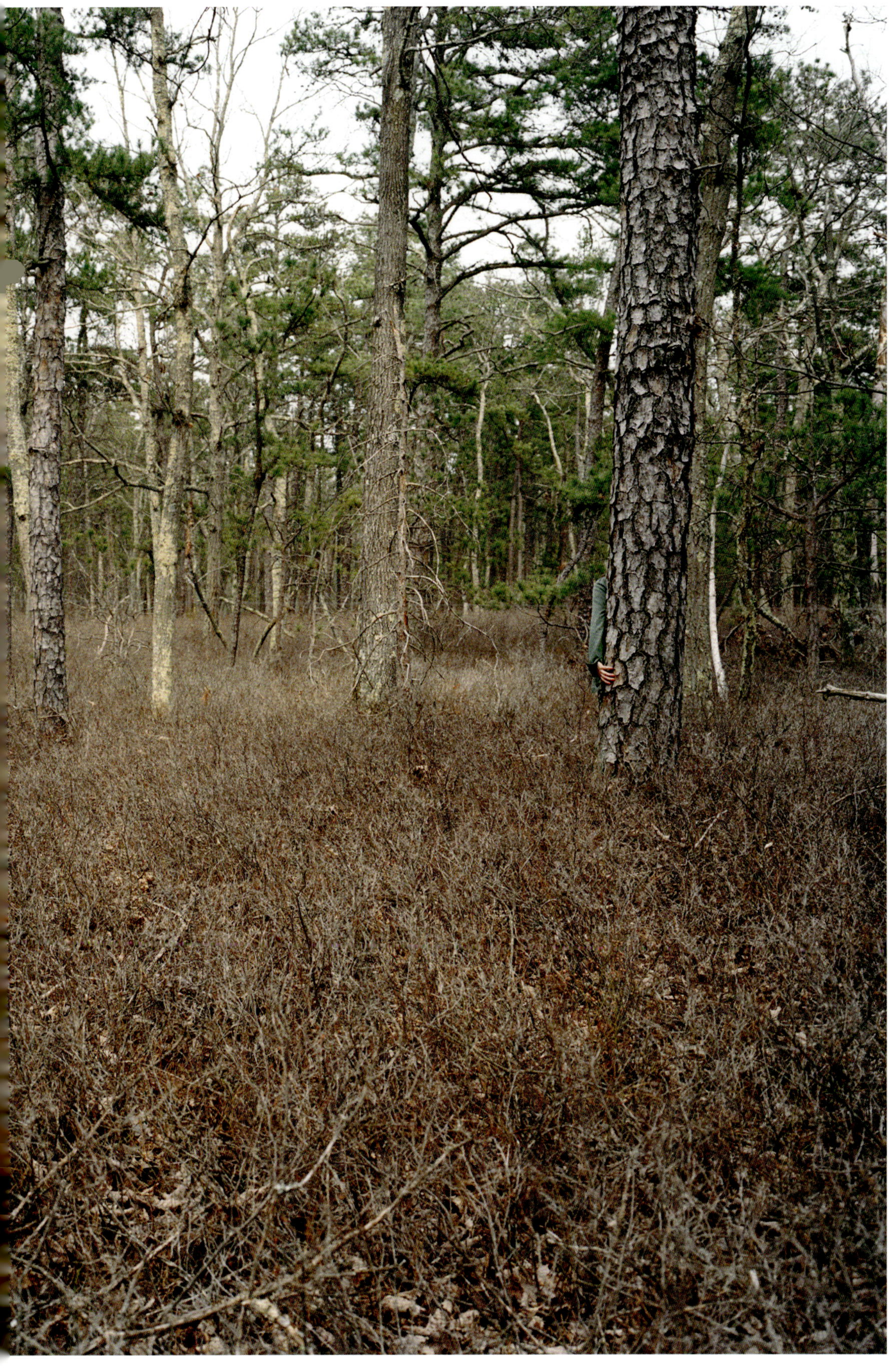

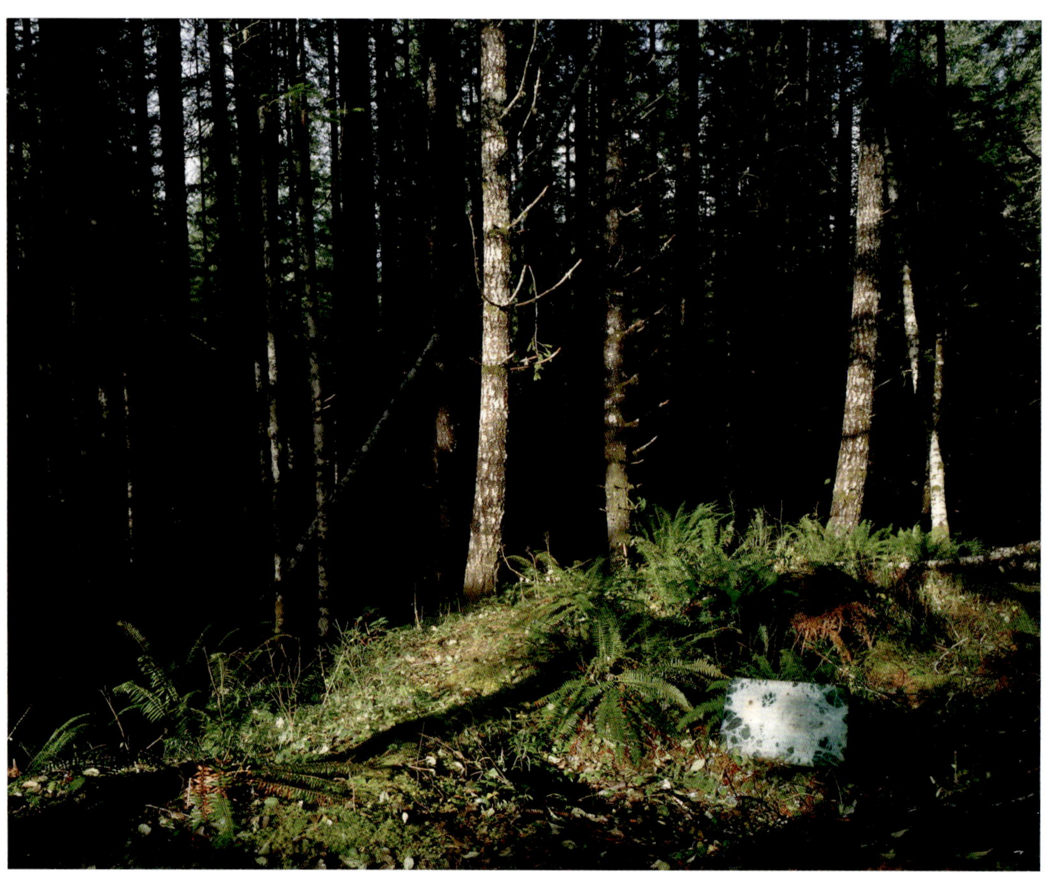

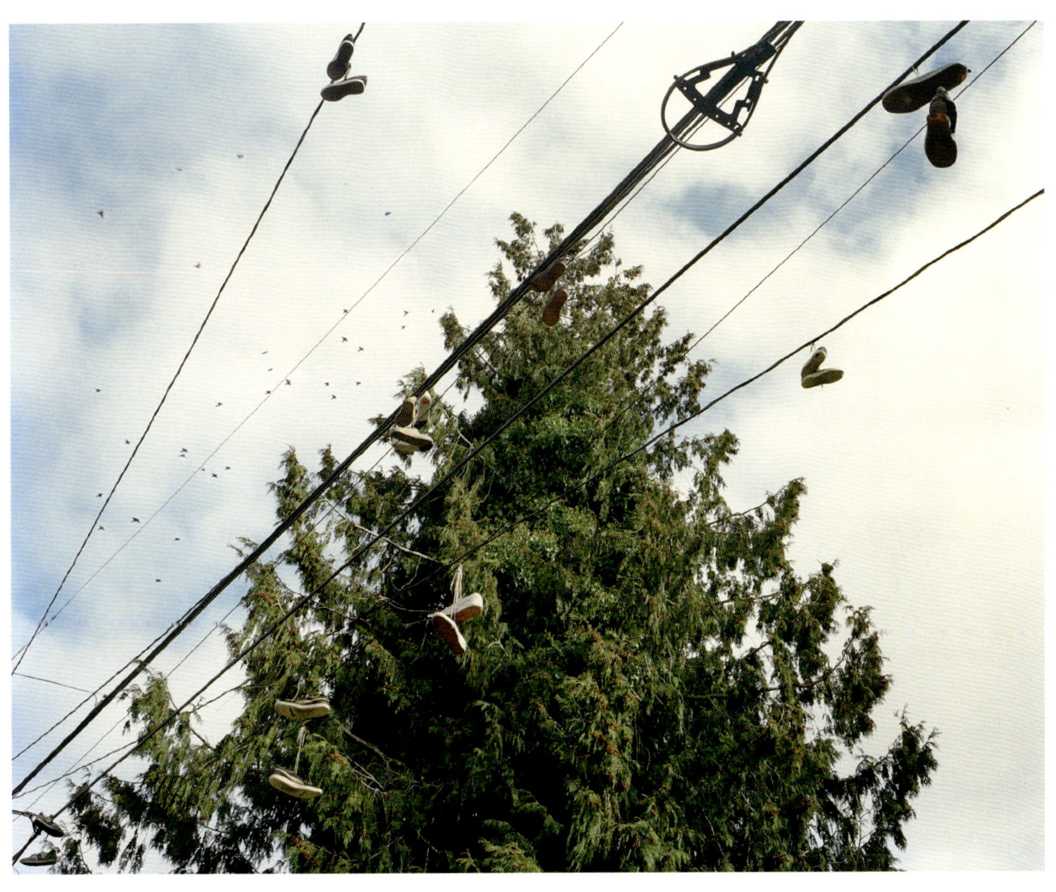

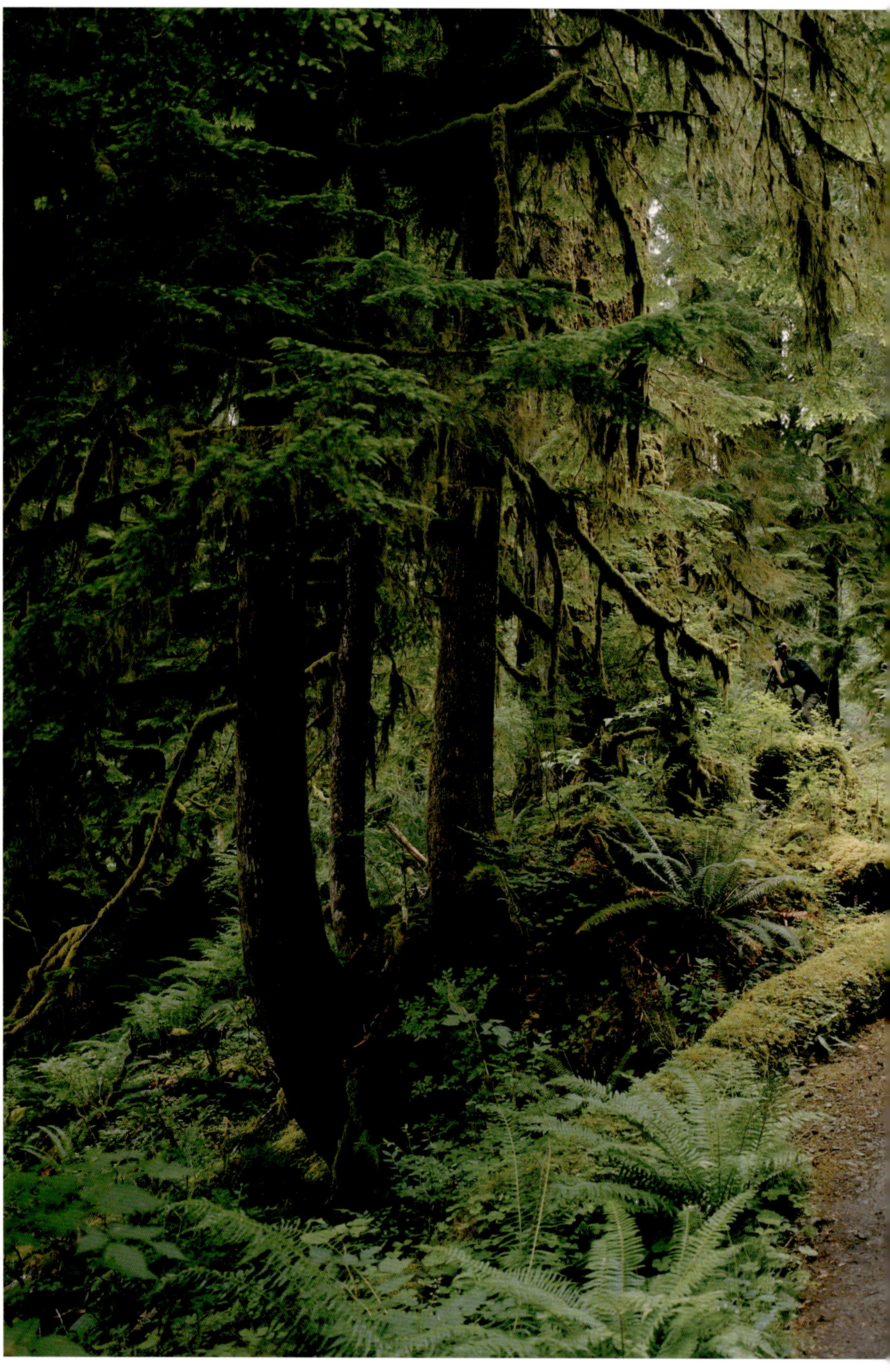

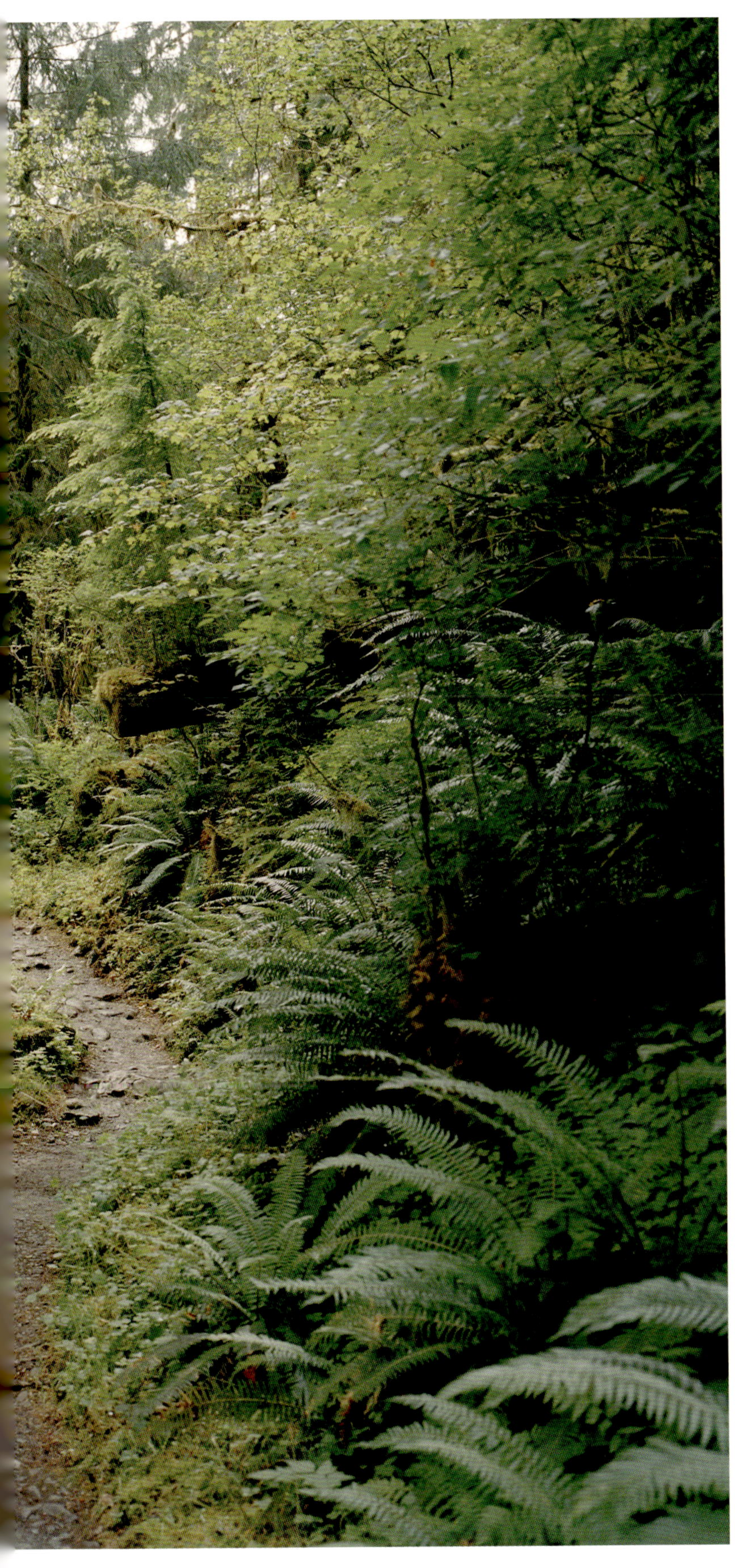

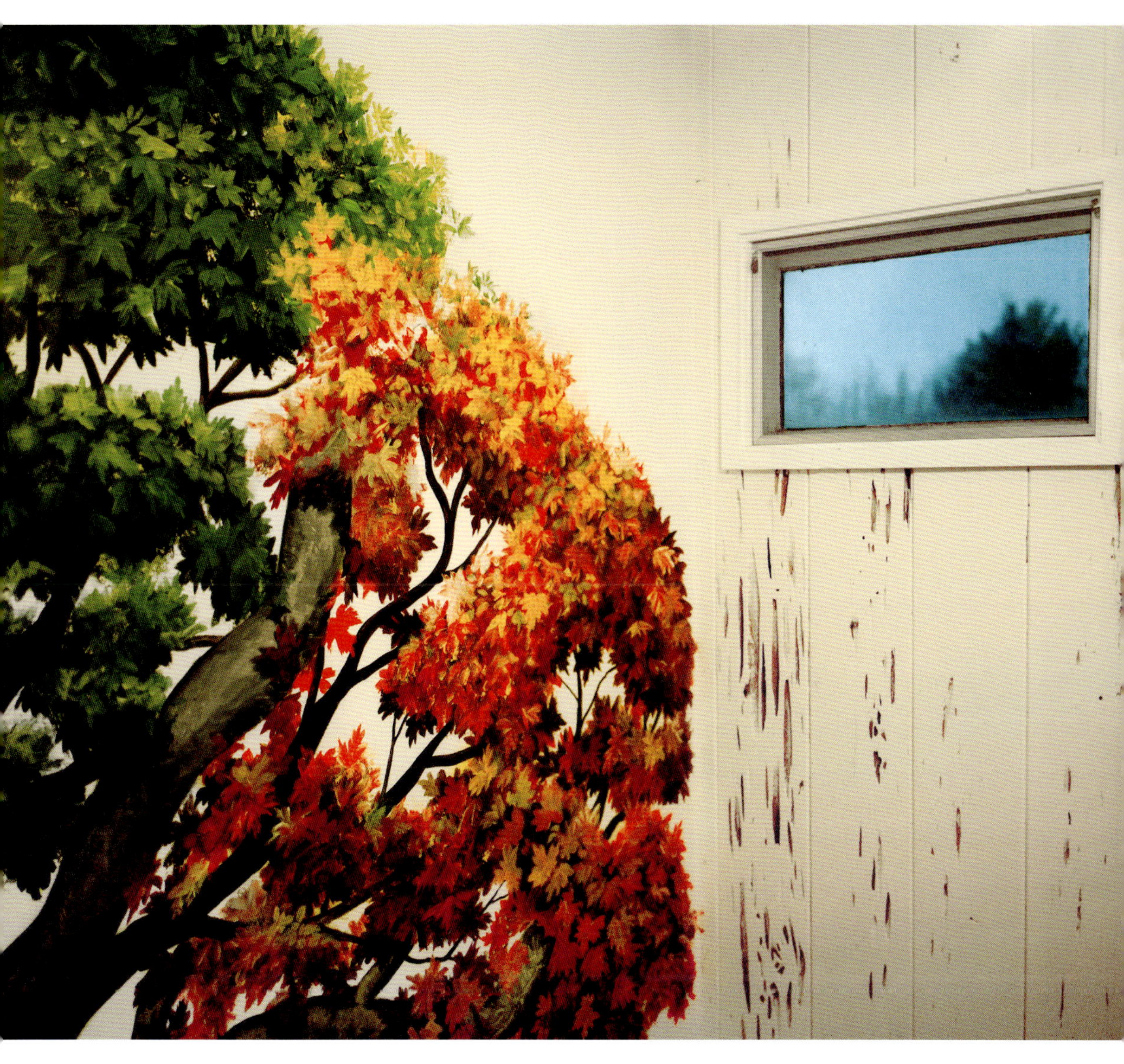

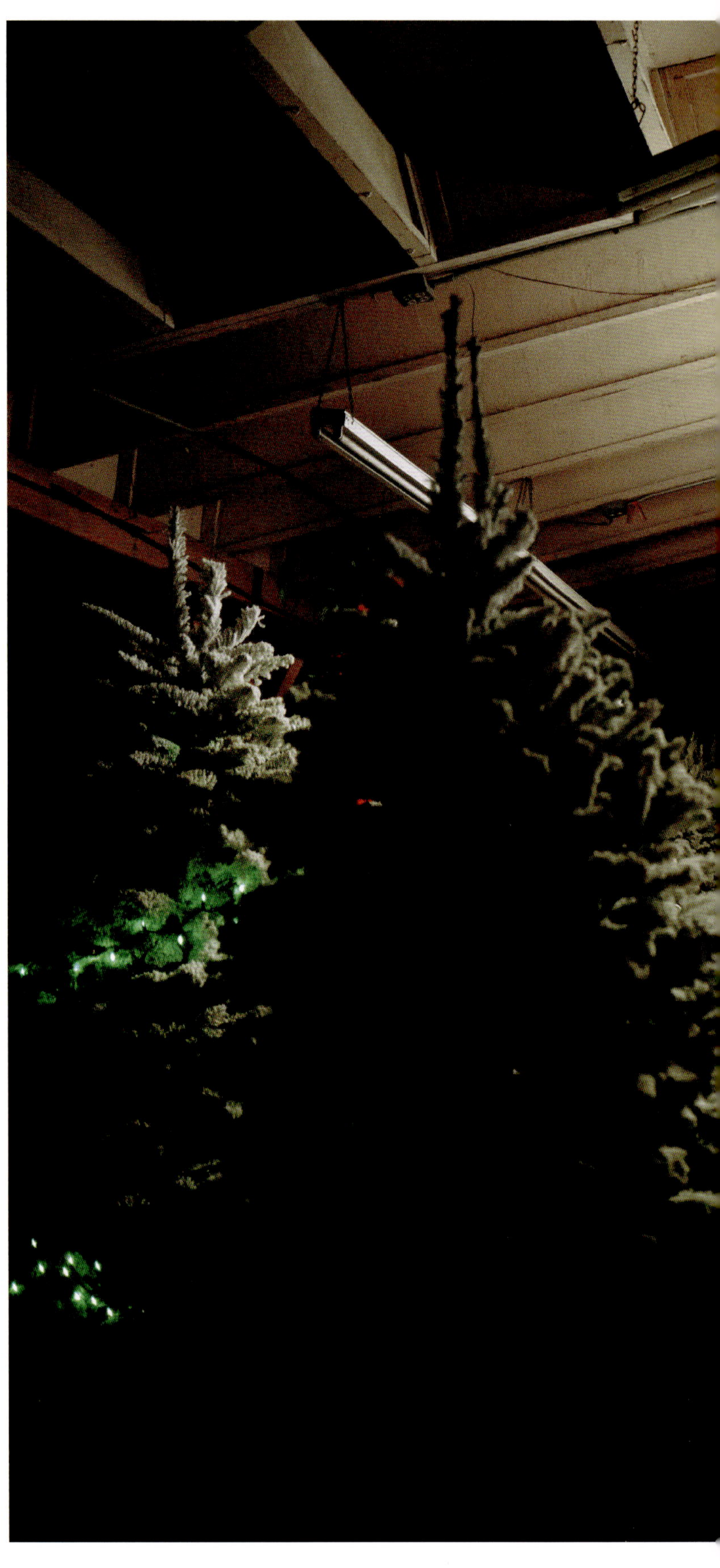

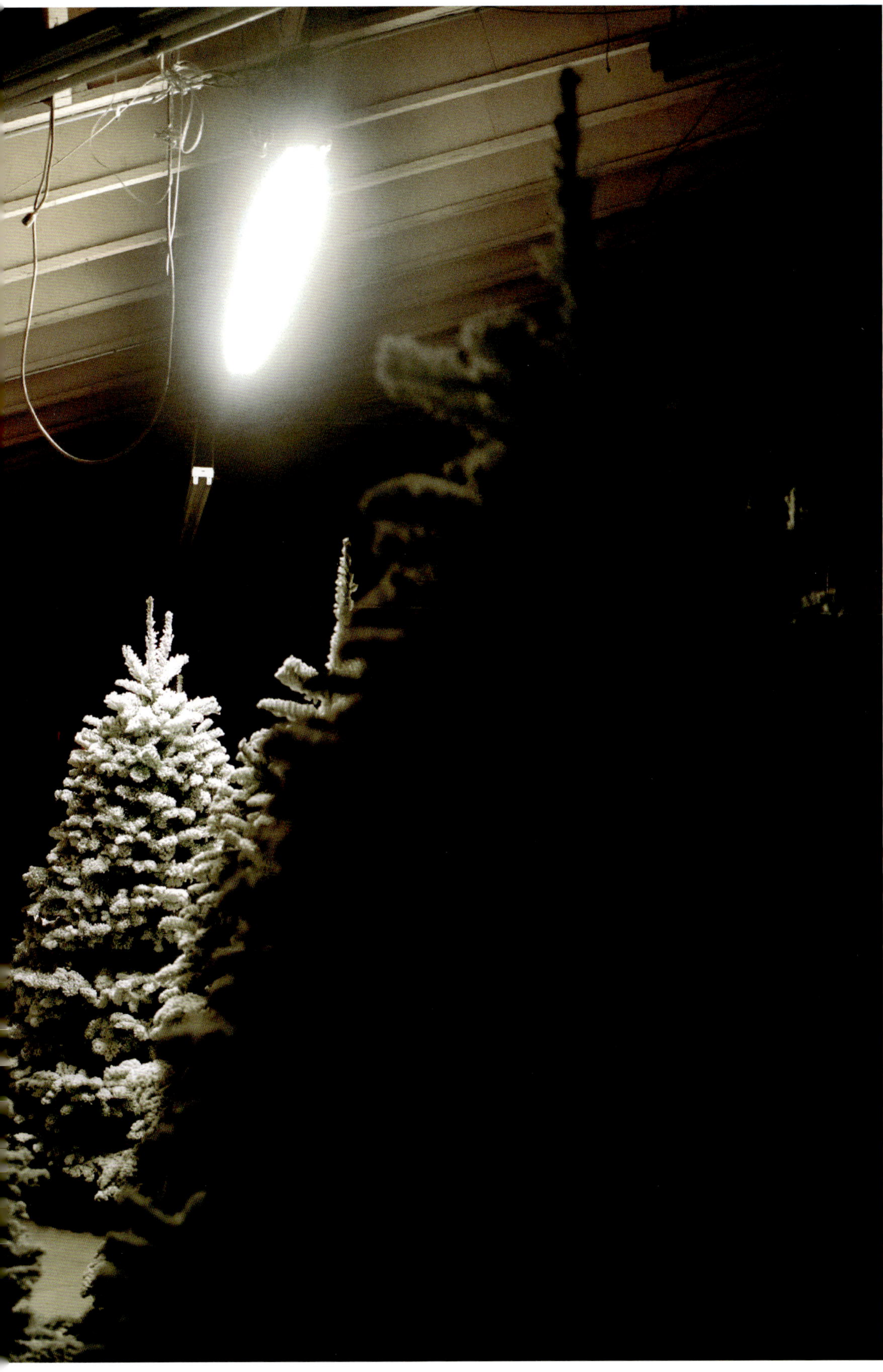

I try to never forget that trees are verbs always headed up. They yearn, they elevate, they rise, they ascend, they have a major sun jones, they set their feet and then jump verrrrrrrrrrrry slowly, like the tallest slenderest toughest rough-skinned quietest basketball players you ever saw.

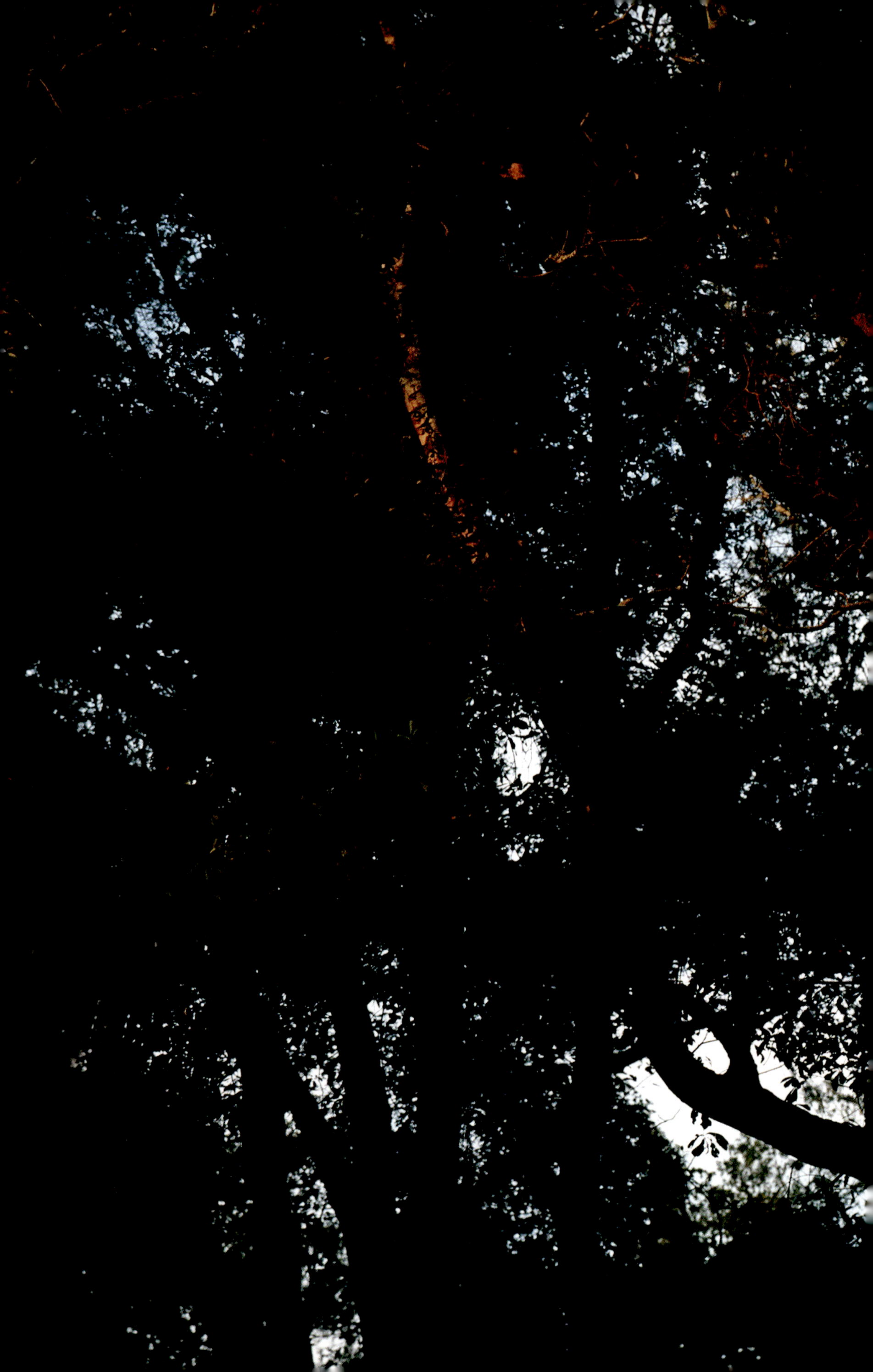

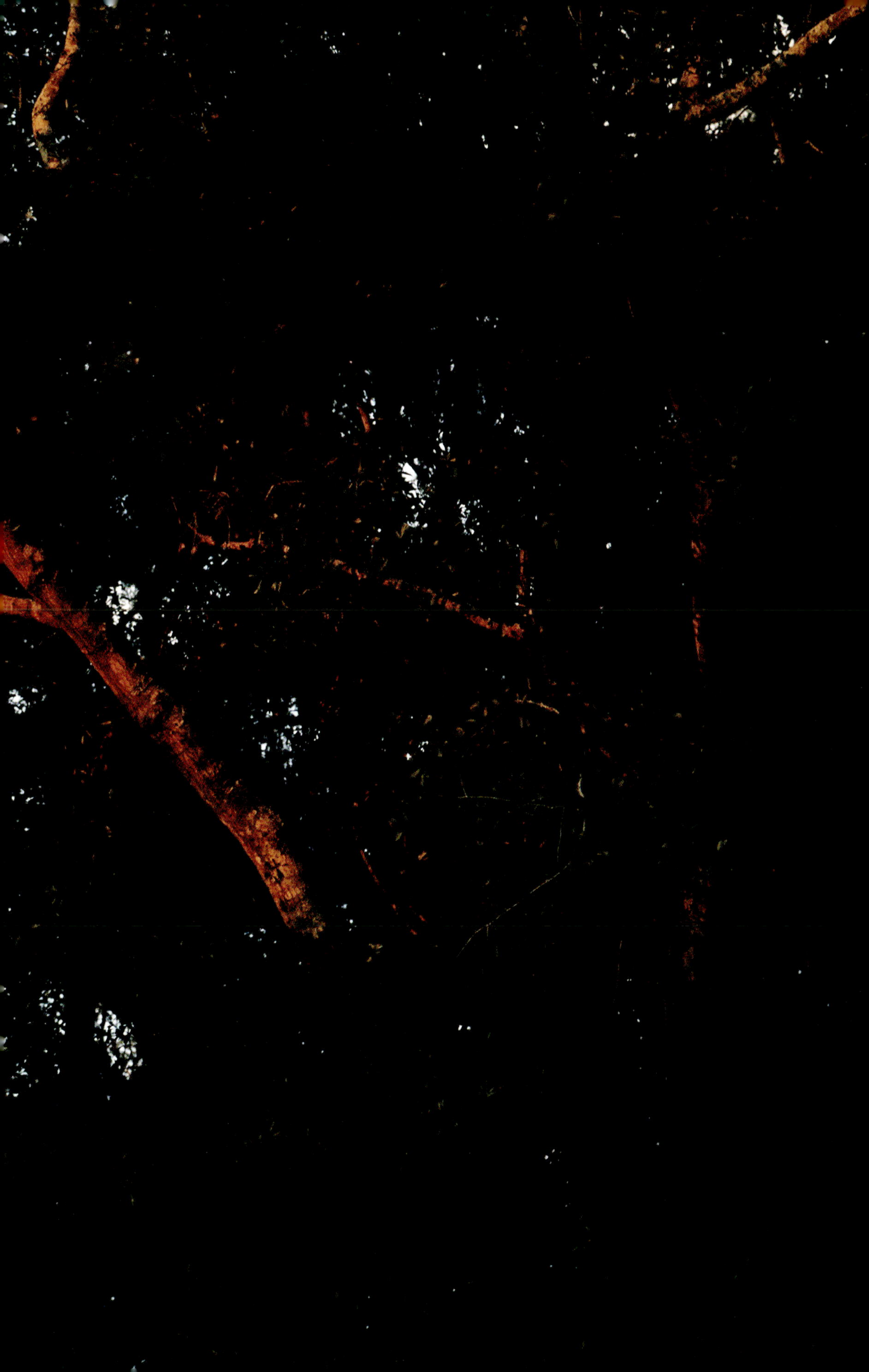

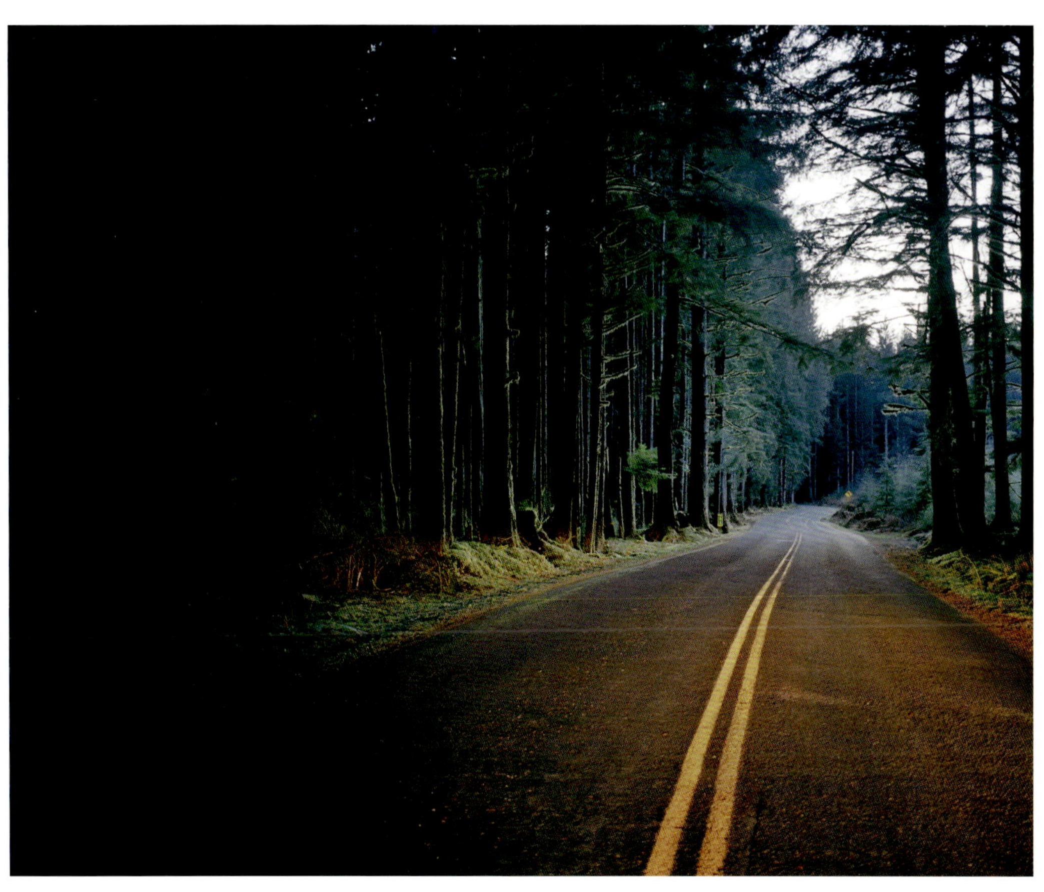

You can't stop the wonder with which people gawk and gape at trees. Even if you know there are no trees beyond the fringe, even if you are absolutely sure of that, even if there's nothing there but the awful battlefield detritus of a clear-cut, you drive along through the trees that are there, gazing at them with respect and awe and affection. They are our cousins, our teammates, our ancient teachers. You can learn a great deal about fit and peace and endurance and dignity and patience from trees.

I have.

INDEX

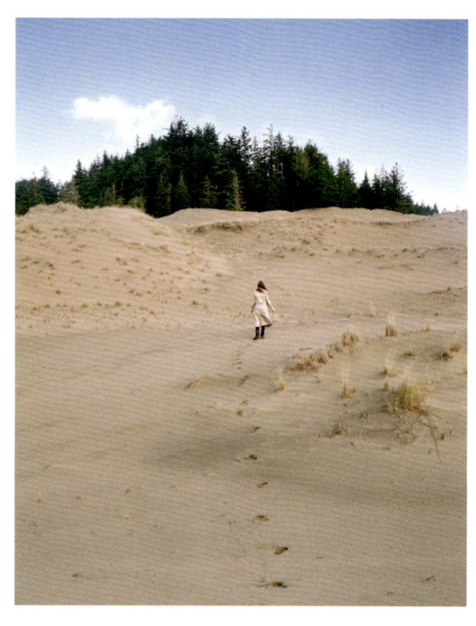

Across cultures and centuries, the forest has occupied a unique place in our collective imagination. Light and dark, good and evil, chaos and peace: these oppositions are as fundamental to the forest's liminal landscape as they are to the human experience.

There are countless histories and myths that involve humankind venturing beyond the structured limit of civilization into the chaotic labyrinth of the woods. Like so many before me, I too went into the woods in search of adventure, transcendence, and the unknown. I entered the forests of the Pacific Northwest because of some ineffable thing connected to memories and mythologies of my own, and continued my quest in other woodlands seeking a more universal understanding of the varied and branching experience of humanity in relation to this primal, mysterious landscape.

While I doubt I will ever be fully out of the woods, for now I have returned from my arboreal outings with *Sylvania*– a composite "forest-land" of photographs comprising scenes from various and sundry American woodlands. Through images of both real and depicted nature, this book examines the differing characteristics of these woods while also seeking the Forest Universal rooted in them all, exploring the physical and metaphoric presence of the forest in the contemporary world.

– Anna Beeke

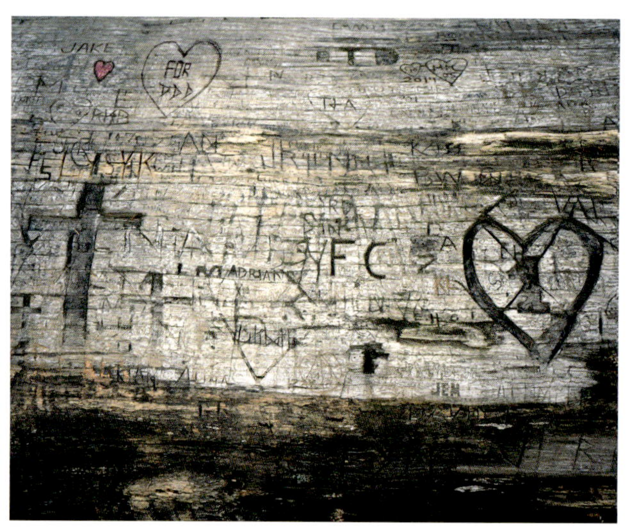
JAKE
FOR
ADRIAN
FC
JEN

ACKNOWLEDGMENTS

Bringing a first book to fruition requires a great deal of support and encouragement, and I am filled with incalculable gratitude toward all the wonderful people who have helped make this possible.

I am deeply grateful to Brian Doyle for his words – for seeing what I am trying to express in my own medium, and for giving it a complementary form in his. Further, I would like to thank him for writing the bewitching novel *Mink River*, which I picked up on San Juan Island in the early stages of shooting *Sylvania* and which became an unexpected muse in my search for the magical undercurrents of reality.

For insight and guidance along the way, I am particularly indebted to Elisabeth Biondi, Elinor Carruci, Marvin Heiferman, Andrew Moore, Gus Powell, Charles Traub, Kiki Bauer, Bonnie Yochelson, and my peers at the School of Visual Arts. Thank you for your candid critique and inspiration.

For supporting the creation of this body of work and its transformation into a book, I am infinitely thankful to the following individuals and institutions: Humble Arts Foundation and LTI/ Lightside, the School of Visual Arts and the SVA Alumni Society, Uprise Art, American Photographic Artists, Douglas Drysdale, Mary Drysdale, Martha Peters, Howard Chua-Eon, Rob Lancefield, Hanna and Jacob Kaufman, Giorgio Furioso, David Carmen, Aidan Joseph, Dov Harel, Torre Johnson, Maxwell Mackenzie and Rebecca Cross, Suzanne Resnick, Peter J. Cohen, John Keon, Amy McIntosh and Jeffrey Toobin, Mary Schmidt, Kaye and Bob Wertz, Michael Dabney, Jim McCarthy, Etan Fraiman, and all the many, many others who pitched in. For your technical savvy, thank you Blake Ogden.

For your persistent love and patience, thank you to my exceptional friends and family. I am particularly grateful to Granddad, Aunt Mary, Leeor, Alia, Corina, Hayley, my annisa family, and of course my wonderful parents – who have unflaggingly encouraged my every whim, and who inadvertently inspired this arboreal adventure.

And finally, to Michael, Taj, and Ursula of Daylight, without whom this book would still be a mere dream – I am forever indebted and eternally grateful for your belief in *Sylvania* and for bringing it to life so beautifully.

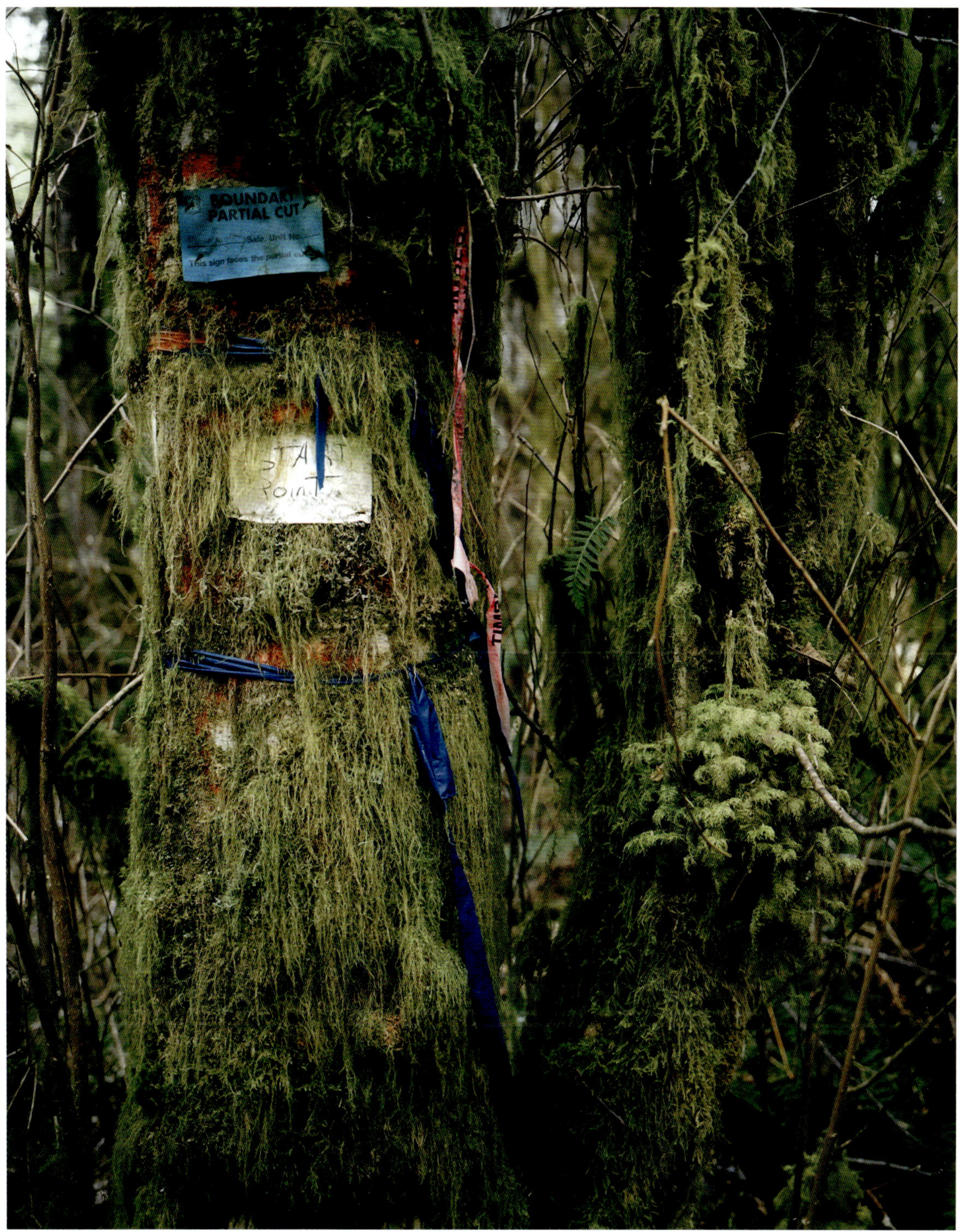
PARTIAL CUT
Sale, Unit
This sign faces the
START
Point